For Love and Forever

A Collection of Short Stories

SLOAN PARKER

Published by
Sloan Parker Press
www.sloanparker.com

For Love and Forever

Cops and Lovers

This story started off as a brief 500-word scenario titled "Partners" and was originally shared via the author's website. It was later revised and expanded into the following novelette.

Sawyer Crenshaw drew in a long breath and leaned back on his elbows. His T-shirt lay crumpled in a ball beside him on the mattress and his jeans were open at the front. He didn't bother to zip up his fly. In a few minutes he and Finn would get back to where they'd been headed.

Who the hell got half-naked, kissed like they'd been doing a minute ago, and then stopped before they got to the fucking? Something was seriously messed up between them. Had been for a while.

Finn stood across the room. He had his back to the wall, his arms folded across his bare chest. He sported a scowl that said everything Sawyer didn't want to hear.

Or maybe he did. Maybe they needed to have this conversation. Get everything out in the open. Finally. Before the incredible tension that had been building between them for the past few months seeped into the job.

Not that either one of them would let that happen. They were damn good cops.

Both served on the department's SWAT team. They'd been friends since the day Finn joined the unit, and as two of the team's few single guys with no kids—and the only gay ones— they spent a lot of nights after work and weekends hanging out at Sawyer's apartment or Finn's house, spending their time off watching movies or lifting weights at the gym or working on one of Finn's many home-improvement projects.

Then eventually they devoted a lot of that time to simply fucking each other.

Although they hadn't slept together in far too long. Now they spent their downtime watching retro TV, shit like those old '70s cops shows. They didn't talk, didn't laugh at the stupid-ass crooks or the retro hairstyles they usually mocked all through the show.

It was awkward and weird and completely fucked up.

From where he still lay on the bed, Sawyer threw Finn a smirk, knowing that alone would piss him off. "You're mad at me."

Finn kept his hard gaze locked on Sawyer's chest. "I'm not mad."

"Screw that, Masters. You've been mad at me since the raid on that house on Pickett. Like it was my fault."

"You got shot. Twice."

"I didn't *ask* the guy to shoot me."

Finn made eye contact for the first time since the kissing ended. "You might as well have. You went at him like you had no training at all."

Sawyer sat up with a jolt. "Are you calling me a shitty cop?"

"No. I'm calling you a reckless one."

"I know you don't mean that." Sawyer sighed in frustration. It hadn't been his abilities—or lack thereof—that had gotten him injured. It was the asshole homeowner and his brother who'd fired on them as they were attempting to execute a search warrant. He got off the bed. Slowly, like he might spook Finn if he moved too fast, he went to stand in front of the younger man. "Just like I knew in that house you'd have my back. Like always."

Finn met Sawyer's gaze again and snorted out a laugh. He didn't let up on the tense posture, though. "You always think you know everything."

Sawyer let out his own terse laugh before he returned to the more serious expression. Maybe too serious, but somewhere deep inside, there was a part of him that ached to hear Finn say the words. Out loud for once. "Just admit it. You're pissed about the shooting because it freaked you out like nothing else on the job ever has." He jabbed a finger at Finn's bare chest. "Because you're in love with me."

Finn's lips parted. He sucked in a shallow, audible breath.

That was enough of a reaction for Sawyer. He reached for Finn and cupped his cheek, then drew him forward until they were back to the kissing, this time their mouths and tongues and bodies coming together slowly, tenderly, all of Finn pressing into him, focused on him with that usual intensity of his. Shit, Sawyer would never tire of kissing this man.

When they finally parted, Finn fell back against the wall. "God, you're infuriating." He smiled with a softness Sawyer had rarely seen from him in the past few months. "And you're right. About everything. So don't ever get your ass shot again."

"Deal." Sawyer gripped Finn by the waistband of his jeans and tugged until he was in his arms again. "So long as you promise me the same thing."

"What?" Finn shrugged out of the embrace. "Not to get shot?"

"Yeah." Sawyer hesitated, unsure if he could actually say the words. How big of a jackass did that make him? He'd known for a long time how he felt about Finn. He'd just never said it to anyone before. Not a lover. Not a friend. And definitely not the woman who'd given birth to him, then practically forgot he existed. He forced himself to meet Finn's penetrating, hopeful stare. "Because you're not the only one in love here."

Finn's eyes widened. He hastily checked the reaction and shook his head. "I never thought you'd admit that."

"What? You think I'm a complete asshole?"

"No. Just the most stubborn one I've ever met." They both laughed that time.

Something shifted in Finn then. His body went tight. He was suddenly on alert, like they were on the job and the commander had just called for lights-out in the tactical wagon, which meant they were twenty seconds out on a raid. Or maybe Finn had just made a startling realization. He pushed away from the wall and stormed past Sawyer, his movements stiff, agitated. When he got to the other side of the room, he came to an abrupt stop. "We have to end this."

"What?" Sawyer's chest tightened. He frowned at Finn's back. Were they having the same conversation?

Finn turned to face him. "Not us." He pointed to the bed. "Not this. The job." He drew in an unsteady breath like this was the hardest thing for him to admit. "I can't work with you any longer. One of us has to leave SWAT."

Sawyer's jaw dropped. He instinctively stormed forward two steps, then jerked to a stop, the bed now between them. "What the fuck? We've worked together for years." Long before they'd started fucking each other. "And it's not like us being together is a recent thing."

"I know. But it's different now. It's been getting more and more complicated." Finn studied the empty bed before him. "All I cared about in that house was getting to you, making sure you were okay." He shifted on his feet as if he wanted to move farther away, only his back was already at the opposite wall. He closed his eyes instead. "It took everything I had just to stay focused for the thirty seconds the team needed to secure the scene. Thirty seconds where I didn't give a fuck about my job." He opened his eyes and smacked his own chest. "Me! I didn't care if the assholes got away."

"So." Sawyer shrugged. "It was one damn moment. A lapse. It would suck to see anyone on the team take a hit like that. Those guys are like our brothers."

"It's different for us. And it's not just going to be that one moment. Not any longer. It's going to be every damn time we head out on a call-out, and you know it."

Sawyer crossed his arms over his chest and held firm. Finn was talking crap. Neither one of them was about to let their personal feelings for each other affect the job or put anyone else at risk. They were both too driven and well-trained for that shit. There was no one Sawyer trusted to have his back more than Finn.

But one look at Finn, and he understood that the man he knew better than anyone wasn't going to back down.

It was the job.

Or it was them.

"Fuck this." Sawyer rounded the bed to Finn. He grabbed him by the back of the neck and yanked him forward until they were eye to eye, their foreheads almost touching. "Don't do this. Neither one of us is walking away from SWAT."

"We have to." Finn shoved him back a step. "And you have to make a choice. You get me in your bed. Or you get me at work. It's that simple."

Simple? Sawyer spun away and ran a hand through his hair as he doubled back across the bedroom. "This is fucked up."

He heard Finn approach behind him. There was a long pause like Finn was waiting for something more from him, but Sawyer couldn't force himself to face him or say another word. Then quietly Finn added, "I know which one I want you to choose, but it has to be something we both want, something we decide together." He waited once more, but when Sawyer said nothing in response, Finn spoke again. "You think it over and let me know." He got moving, going past Sawyer and out into the hall, then out of the apartment, closing the door behind him.

Sawyer stared down at the balled-up T-shirt lying on his bed, a reminder of what they never got to that night, what they might never get to again if he made the choice to end things between them and keep working together instead.

Like that was any kind of choice. There was no way he could give up the job. It was who he was. Who they both were. But give up Finn?

"Fuck!" He grabbed the T-shirt off the bed and flung it at the open doorway where Finn had walked out.

Goddamn him.

* * * *

That night Sawyer lay alone in his bed, staring at the dark ceiling above. For once in his life, he'd taken a chance when it came to his heart. He'd let someone in, even admitted how he felt, and now…

"Fuck." He rolled onto his hip and punched the pillow on the other side of the bed, the one Finn slept on when he stayed over.

Why the hell did the fucker have to say anything about

leaving SWAT or give him such a screwed-up ultimatum? Finn
was making his reaction to the shooting in that house on Pickett
sound worse than it had been. He had to be. They'd always put
the job first when they were on duty. Neither one of them would
let anything get in the way of doing what they were both damn
good at. Protect and serve. It was their life.

Sawyer grabbed the now balled-up pillow, dragged it to him,
and buried his face in the fabric. It smelled of Finn's cologne,
crisp and clean.

With that scent, Sawyer was back to the night everything
changed between them, the night he'd never forget.

He closed his eyes and let himself fall into the memory.

* * * *

Two years earlier...

Sawyer watched in silence as Finn threw his truck into park,
cut the engine, and shoved the driver's side door open with his
shoulder. He was out like a shot. He slammed the door shut,
then stormed up the sidewalk to the house.

Sawyer had never seen Finn that pissed off. It was kind of
amusing. He let out a laugh in the empty cab of the truck. Better
to get that out now. No way was he going to have that reaction
in close proximity to Finn. He'd get his nuts squeezed off in
response. Finn might just be the most easygoing guy on SWAT,
but once he got pushed too far, he would never back down.
Most likely that came from being a member of such a big
family. Four brothers and two sisters, Finn stuck right in the
middle of the pack. He'd probably had to fight his way through
a lot of battles for his fair share of everything.

It just took a lot to get him to the point of no return.

Sawyer grabbed the bag of tacos they'd gotten at a drive-
through on the way home and followed Finn inside. Ever since
Finn had joined SWAT a few years earlier, they'd spent a lot of
their downtime together, and eventually they started sharing
rides to work and eating dinner together nearly every night.

Before Finn, Sawyer hadn't had any friends outside of work.

He didn't connect with people easily. Hanging with Finn was effortless, no need to screw around with small talk or pretend to be anything but who they were. Even though Sawyer would give his life for any one of his brothers on SWAT, there was a lingering unease that came with hanging around straight guys. Like he just knew they were always, somewhere in the back of their minds, wondering what he did in bed with a guy, dying to know if he liked to suck dick, if he took it up the ass.

But with Finn, it was uncomplicated, normal. A real friendship. Which was probably why they'd never crossed that invisible line and jumped into bed together, no matter how tempting it would be to land a steady fuck buddy like that.

Sawyer closed the side door of Finn's house behind him and stepped into the kitchen. Finn was pulling glasses and plates from a cupboard near the sink, moving with clear agitation. Sawyer set the bag of food down on the counter beside him. "You okay?"

"Sure. I'm great. Fantastic." Finn ditched the plates onto the counter, practically slamming them down and breaking both in the process. He turned to glare at Sawyer. "How the hell do you think I feel?"

"Hey." Sawyer held up his hands as he took a step back. "I'm not the enemy here."

"Then keep your lame-ass questions to yourself."

"Fine, but that guy was just trying to goad you. He was hoping you'd take a swing at him."

"I know that. I'm not an idiot."

The reporter who was writing a feature article about their SWAT unit had been trailing the team for the past two weeks and had taken it upon himself to target Finn with a level of hostility he was not directing at anyone else. Sawyer's guess was that the guy was trying to provoke Finn into some sort of testosterone-induced rage that would make a great angle for his article. *SWAT Cop Explodes on the Job.* Anything to sell more papers.

Maybe it was because the reporter had once known a guy who looked like Finn, maybe a bully back in school or someone who'd gotten a job over him. Whatever the reason, it was fucked up. Finn didn't deserve that kind of shit aimed at him. But...

Sawyer arched his brows. "All I gotta say is, it was a good thing he picked you to go after."

Finn threw him another hard look. "What the fuck does that mean?"

Sawyer shrugged. "You didn't lose it with him. Not sure any of the rest of us would've managed that after all the crap he said to you."

"Well, I have no intention of getting written up. Or worse. All because of that asshole." He went to the fridge and grabbed a two-liter bottle of soda, then turned to Sawyer again with a pointed stare. "Or any asshole."

Wait. Was that directed at him? "What are you talking about?"

"You want to pretend the other night didn't happen? Fine. Two can play at that game." He ditched the bottle on the counter and picked up the bag of tacos like he was going to dish them out onto the plates. Instead he chucked the bag back onto the counter. "I'm not hungry." He stormed past Sawyer and headed out of the kitchen, anger radiating off him as he went.

What the hell? Sawyer trailed after him. By the time he reached Finn's bedroom at the end of the hall, Finn was at his open closet door. He already had his shirt and jeans off and was standing there in nothing but a pair of black briefs that perfectly hugged his toned ass.

Holy fuck. Sawyer had seen him with his shirt off every day while they were roofing Finn's house that summer, seen him dressing numerous times in the locker room at work and likewise at the gym, but this... Finn Masters nearly naked in the man's own bedroom.

Desire raced through Sawyer with a sudden fierceness that left his mouth hanging open. He just stood there panting, gaping at those black briefs—and the man underneath—his blood rushing to his cock with a jolt.

Finn turned and stopped short when he spotted Sawyer. For a long moment, they held the stare, a spark of something new and unbridled passing between them. Then Finn's gaze hardened. "Get the hell out of my house."

That was it. Sawyer started for him. "What is wrong with you?"

All at once Finn had both arms up. He shoved at Sawyer's chest. "I told you to fucking get out."

Sawyer gripped Finn's wrists before he could get in another shove. That must've sufficiently pissed Finn off. He twisted his arms free and sent a fist barreling for Sawyer's face.

Sawyer ducked the hit and got Finn backed against the wall by the closet door in a flash. "What in the goddamn hell is wrong with you?"

"I'm sick of this shit." Finn struggled against Sawyer's hold.

"What? That reporter?"

Finn stopped. "No, shithead. You."

"What are you talking about?"

With another burst of energy, Finn broke Sawyer's hold and grasped him by the upper arms. He spun them around and shoved Sawyer to the wall. The drawers of the dresser beside them and the glass bottles of cologne sitting on top rattled in response. Finn didn't hesitate. He got in Sawyer's face, his lips almost touching Sawyer's, their bodies nearly connecting at every point along their lengths. "I want you." Anger still alive in his expression, he ground his groin against Sawyer's, and Sawyer had to bite back the moan. Finn narrowed his eyes at him. "And I *know* you want me."

What could he say to that? Deny that for weeks now he'd been having the most erotic dreams about them fucking each other? Dreams he'd been trying to tell himself meant nothing? Because that would be the first time he'd ever lied to Finn.

Finn repeated the action, rubbing the heavy bulge hidden under those black briefs against the front of Sawyer's jeans. "You almost kissed me the other night. Sitting right there on my damn couch."

"So?"

"So, you think it's going to be easy to push aside what you want?"

"Yeah." He had to. Didn't he?

Finn searched Sawyer's face for a long moment. Then he dropped his arms and stepped back. "Okay." He watched him for another few seconds, the anger and frustration dissipating. Something much more like disappointment followed. He turned for the door.

"Where are you going?"

With a glance back over his shoulder, Finn said, dryly, much too evenly, "To eat tacos." He continued toward the hallway.

Fuck that. Sawyer was across the room in three steps. He crowded Finn face-first to the wall by the bedroom door. He leaned in until the arousal he couldn't ignore at the front of his jeans was tight to Finn's ass. He pressed his lips to Finn's ear. "Fuck yeah, I want you. Like you wouldn't believe."

Finn gasped in response. He reached around with one arm and gripped Sawyer's ass. "So do it."

That time it was Sawyer who worked his cock against Finn. He propped both of his hands on the wall, one on each side of Finn's shoulders, and humped against him like he was trying to get inside him, and they still had the jeans and briefs in the way. He was practically grunting in Finn's ear with each shift of his hips, Finn driving back to meet him with as much force.

Then Finn let go of him and went for those black briefs like he was going to tug them out of the way.

Sawyer didn't think. He stopped Finn's movements and slid a hand under his chin, turning Finn's head to the side. He wanted him, but not just to fuck. He wanted it all. He plastered his lips to Finn's, hoping to hell Finn wasn't going to pummel him in response.

He didn't. Finn wrapped a hand around the back of Sawyer's head and held on. He parted his lips and slid his tongue into the touch, deepening the kiss, feeding him what felt like months of desire and need into that one silky, wet press of their mouths.

Sawyer had never been kissed like that. Not once.

He was going to lose it with just Finn's lips on his. He pulled back. "Need to…"

"Yeah." Finn went for his underwear again.

Sawyer slapped his hand out of the way and grasped the briefs himself, tugging them down Finn's legs, planting kiss after kiss on all that firm, solid skin as he went, finally getting the chance to explore the body he'd been dreaming about for weeks. He ran his lips and tongue over the warm flesh of Finn's lower back, his ass cheeks, the backs of his thighs, all the while breathing in his scent.

When he had the underwear down to Finn's calves, he stood straight. Finn kicked the briefs off the rest of the way while Sawyer got his own jeans open and his dick out. Only then did he realize what else they needed.

He swore under his breath, managed to grunt out one word. "Condom."

Finn pointed to the nightstand by the bed, his arm shaking with the gesture. Sawyer forced himself to step away and went for the drawer. He found condoms and lube, grabbed both. By the time he was back to Finn, Sawyer had the condom on and his erection slicked up with the lube.

Finn was still facing the wall, his forehead pressed to it, both hands flat to the surface. He was breathing heavily, his entire upper body shifting with each harsh inhale. "Hurry."

"Am." Sawyer laughed as he leaned into Finn. "Who knew you'd be this bossy?" Not that he cared. He loved it, loved Finn sounding—and looking—so desperate. All because it was Sawyer who was about to get inside him.

As if to confirm that thought, Finn stuck his ass out, spread his legs, making room for Sawyer.

Sawyer dropped his forehead to Finn's shoulder, trying to calm down so he didn't embarrass himself and explode on contact. Another deep breath. He couldn't wait one more second. He lifted his head and drove forward. Finn's ass swallowed the tip of his cock, and Sawyer had to stop again. The tight grip of heat encasing the head of his dick was almost more than he could take.

Finn was breathing harder. "God, Sawyer. Don't hold back."

So he didn't. He thrust his hips forward, then repeated the action again and again, setting a pace in and out like a man on a mission, fucking Finn against the wall.

Not that Finn seemed to mind. He clawed at the surface

before him, groaned with each slam of their bodies, with each stab of Sawyer's dick inside his ass.

"Shit." This wasn't going to last long. Sawyer jerked his hips faster, harder. "Gonna…" Oh fuck, was he ever. He plunged into Finn one last time and came, his body plastered to Finn, holding on to him as he shuddered through the spike of release.

When he finally stilled and the intense pleasure eased, he collapsed against Finn. "Holy hell. That was…" He breathed deep. He had no words.

"Uh-huh." Finn sounded tense with need.

Sawyer ditched the condom, grabbed Finn by the upper arms, and spun him around. He captured Finn's mouth in another kiss, taking him in hand at the same time. He stroked his length, tightening and twisting his grip at the head of Finn's erection, all the while never letting up on the kiss. Then he got his hand moving faster, sending it flying over Finn's cock.

Finn threw his head back to the wall and arched into the touch. "Fuck, yes!" Apparently that really did it for him.

If he liked that…

Sawyer dropped to his knees. This part he was damn good at. He swallowed Finn's cock in one lunge. Hearing Finn's guttural moan in response was all the encouragement Sawyer needed. He wanted to make this so damn good for him.

Yet it was something else too.

He wanted more than this one moment. So much more.

A few minutes later, as Finn gripped the back of his head and exploded in his mouth with another drawn-out groan that included Sawyer's name in the mix, Sawyer knew that if he had anything to say about it, they were both going to get more.

A hell of a lot more.

* * * *

Sawyer awoke the next morning from a restless sleep filled with dreams of that first night with Finn. He lay there hard and wanting, but there was also a lingering sorrow that he couldn't shake, and it overshadowed everything. He didn't even bother to take himself in hand. Instead he rolled his head to the side and took note of the still-empty pillow beside him.

"Damn him."

He forced himself to look away and glanced at the clock. Five a.m. He so didn't need to be up this early. He should try to get more sleep, but that might mean more dreams. No way in hell was he going there.

He got up and paused to sit at the edge of the bed, giving himself a minute to fully wake up. There was no need to rush. The entire SWAT team wasn't on until later. They were scheduled for a series of night raids. The unit was typically on call 24-7, but since call-outs weren't an everyday occurrence, they usually went in on first shift to keep up with their rigorous training, work crime suppression, or assist with specialized training for the rest of the division.

Not that day, though. He had twelve hours until he had to be in. How the hell was he going to keep himself busy all day? And keep his mind off Finn and his ridiculous ultimatum?

A task that turned out to be impossible. The day dragged.

He went through the e-mail he'd been letting pile up in his in-box, deleted the spam, scrubbed out the bathroom shower that he hadn't bothered with in weeks, and cleaned out his neglected fridge. After he had the full garbage bag tied up, he glanced at the clock. Ten a.m. Great. Seven more hours.

When he finally got on duty that night, he was tired and crabby. He didn't talk to a soul as he made his way to his locker and checked his gear. The scheduled raids were minor shit, but a call-out could go bad at any moment. He needed to get his head in the game.

Easier to do if he'd gotten more sleep, if some asshole had just kept his damn mouth shut the night before and let them get to the fucking. Then he'd at least be rid of the sexual frustration he'd been sporting for months now. He and Finn hadn't slept together since before the shooting. Not once through his recovery, the rehab, and now this weirdness between them. He'd be feeling a hell of a lot better right then if he'd finally gotten laid the night before.

Right. Like the mammoth amount of tension pressing down on his chest had anything to do with sex, no matter how long it had been since he'd had Finn in his bed.

The locker room door opened, and their SWAT commander

walked in. "Evening, everyone." Weston, as he preferred the team to call him, stood stiff and straight as he surveyed the room, making eye contact with each man, his usual routine before a call-out. "We'll be one man short tonight."

Sawyer glanced around the room. That one man was Finn. Where the fuck was he?

"Briefing in ten," Weston added, then turned to leave.

Sawyer trailed the commander out. "Where's Masters?"

Weston kept on moving down the hall as he talked. "On vacation."

"He's off tonight?"

"That's what vacation means. He was going to lose the days if he didn't take them, so I let him have two weeks off." Weston went into his office.

Finn followed him inside. "Two weeks? With no notice? Last I heard, he was just gonna let the extra days go."

"Guess he changed his mind." The commander sat behind his desk and eyed Sawyer with suspicion. "He earned those vacation days. They're his to take."

"Sure." Although it wasn't that straightforward. What the hell was Finn doing?

Weston kept the stare going. "You okay, Crenshaw?"

"Yeah."

"You better be. It's going to be a long night. Vice has us scheduled for back-to-back raids."

Sawyer resented the implication that he'd let anything get in the way of the job. Weston was beginning to sound like Finn. Sawyer gave the commander a nod. "I'm ready." He got moving for his locker.

But Weston was right about one thing. It *was* going to be a long night.

* * * *

"Open the goddamn door, Finn." Sawyer repeatedly banged the side of his fist on the wood surface. He didn't care if he woke up the entire block. He and Finn were talking this out. Now.

Finn's house was a yellow bungalow situated on the same quiet street where Finn had grown up. He was still close with his entire family. His siblings, aunts and uncles, cousins, the whole lot of them. Whereas Sawyer wanted nothing to do with the fucked-up family or the twisted childhood he'd tried hard to forget.

Another bang with his fist, and the door flew open. Finn stood there, dark stubble on his face, wearing jeans and nothing else, even his feet bare. "Would you shut the hell up? It's the middle of the damn night. You're gonna piss off my neighbors."

"I don't give a shit." Sawyer pushed past Finn and went inside. "Where were you tonight?"

"Here. I decided to take my vacation."

"Why? Are you going somewhere?"

Finn shut the door and faced Sawyer. "No."

"So you're just gonna stay here alone in your house for two weeks?"

"I'm going to remodel the bathroom like I've been talking about doing. Even started working on retiling the floor tonight."

"Sure. The team goes out on three drug raids, putting their lives on the line, and you're here messing with tile and grout and shit? Makes total sense."

"Fuck you." He started forward like he was going to pass by and head down the hall without another word.

Sawyer grabbed Finn's arm and got him stopped. "Why weren't you there?"

"I can't do it anymore." Finn jerked his arm out of Sawyer's grip. "I'm retiling my bathroom floor so you'll have time and space to think."

"Me?"

"Yeah, you. You're the one who's gotta make up his mind."

"Why are you putting all this on my shoulders?"

"Because I've already made up mine. One of us has to leave the job if we want to keep things going between the sheets."

Sawyer shook his head in disbelief. If Finn thought one of them had to walk away from SWAT, then fine, let Finn do it. He cringed at the thought, though, and kept it quiet because Finn quitting sounded as bad as Sawyer leaving himself. He couldn't stand the thought of Finn not being there every day, not doing something he was meant to do.

As if in answer to an unspoken question, Finn added, "I can't make this call alone. It's not just my life."

"You're damn right it's not." Sawyer turned away and stormed into the kitchen. He knew Finn's place as well as his own apartment. He went to the fridge and reached for a Corona. He held the cold bottle in his fist but paused with the beer still sitting on the shelf. If he started knocking them back, he wasn't going to stop. He was too damn pissed and confused and horny. Losing all that to the buzz of about six beers sounded good. Too good.

He grabbed a bottle of soda instead and chugged half of it down before he slammed the refrigerator door closed and spun around. Finn stood at the kitchen doorway. Shit, he looked good. His sculpted arms were folded over that broad, bare chest, and the worn jeans rode low on his lean hips, showcasing his stellar set of abs. An incredible body trained in tactical firearms, live fire entries, and hand-to-hand combat.

Sawyer tightened his grip on the bottle of soda. He wanted to walk over there, grab the man, drag him down the hall to the bedroom, and forget everything else. Instead, he rested his ass against the kitchen counter, hoping the contact would ground him to that spot before he made a stupid move he couldn't take back.

They stared each other down. There was a hard edge to Finn's expression, but the longer they kept their gazes locked, the more the look in Finn's eyes softened, became something Sawyer was intimately familiar with. Finn unfolded his arms and took a step forward.

Sawyer held up a hand. "Don't."

Finn stopped. "What?"

"You get any closer, I'm not going to be able to think straight."

"Maybe I don't want you thinking straight." Finn smirked and started for him again.

"Stop."

Finn didn't. And Sawyer knew this wasn't going to end well. He couldn't take getting another go with Finn if that was all he was ever going to have, couldn't stand thinking it would be the last time he'd ever get to kiss him, touch him, find himself buried in that amazing ass. Knowing it was the end would make every single moment they were in each other's arms too damn intense.

Apparently Finn didn't care. He'd already changed tactics and was now a man on a mission. He halted before Sawyer, took the bottle of soda from him, and set it aside. He leaned in and propped his hands on the counter on either side of Sawyer, trapping him in place. That look of lust and longing was still there in Finn's eyes. "I want you. Like I've never wanted anyone. Even after all this time together."

Sawyer didn't respond, didn't make a move, but his resolve was fading fast. He looked away and let out an unsteady exhale. He met Finn's stare again, and for the first time since he'd known the man, he saw a desperate plea in those brown eyes staring back at him.

That was it. Nothing could stop Sawyer now. He gripped Finn by the waist and hauled him forward. The kiss was explosive, stubble scratching stubble, their lips and tongues joining again and again.

Finn held Sawyer's face in both hands and pressed him to the counter, taking his mouth in another captivating kiss.

They clutched at each other, rocked body against body, fought for dominance with the kiss, neither letting up. Finn ran both hands down Sawyer's body, then up his torso, lifting his T-shirt as he went. He raised it over Sawyer's head, and the fabric got tangled up.

Finn held the shirt where it was wrapped around Sawyer's wrists and laughed. "I should tie you to my bed like this until you make up your mind."

Sawyer snorted out a laugh. "Don't even think about it." They'd tried the handcuffs thing once. Only it had been Finn secured to Sawyer's headboard, and it had been hot as hell. Sawyer wouldn't actually mind trying it the other way around sometime, but not right then. Not when there was a chance they wouldn't get to do this again. He wanted to feel every inch of Finn. He wanted to kiss his bare flesh, explore with hands and mouth and tongue. He wanted to feel Finn's body arching up under him as he sank into him, as he thrust inside Finn again and again. Nothing was getting in the way of that.

Finn threw him a wicked grin. "Keeping you trapped in my bed for days on end sounds like the perfect vacation to me." Despite his words, he gave in and tugged Sawyer's T-shirt off the rest of the way.

They kissed again, this time their bare chests pressed together. With his arms free, Sawyer swept his hands down Finn's sides, taking in every inch of his masculine, muscular body. Finn didn't have an ounce of fat on him, and it was heady touching all that firm flesh, feeling all those defined muscles jump and flex under his touch.

That contact alone had Sawyer already aching for release, and they were still in their damn jeans. He slid a hand between them and groaned when his palm made contact with the thick bulge of Finn's erection.

Then abruptly, swiftly Finn stepped back, out of Sawyer's reach. "No." He shook his head as if he had to rid himself of the desire before he could say another word. "We can't."

Sawyer tried to move forward, but Finn held both arms up, keeping him at bay. Sawyer stopped. "What the hell? You started this."

Finn took another step back and folded his arms over his chest. "I want an answer first."

"What? Or it's no sex? Who knew you'd play it like that?"

"This isn't some fucked-up game I'm playing with you." He ran a shaking hand over his close-cropped hair. "I can't handle it."

"Handle what?"

"Being with you, knowing it could be the last time."

"It doesn't have to be. That's your deal."

"And I won't take it back. I *can't* take it back." He swung an arm toward the kitchen doorway. "I need you to leave until you've made up your mind."

Fuck that. Sawyer got in Finn's face. "It's a bullshit choice. One of us has to walk away from our job? A job we've worked our asses off to get? A job we love doing? One we're both damn good at? That's not going to happen."

"It has to. Or we're done."

"All because I got shot?" He was shouting now.

"All because I nearly put our teammates in jeopardy. All because you mean too much to me. I can't compartmentalize it anymore. And that's too big of a risk. To us. To the team. To civilians. I'm a good enough cop to know that."

Sawyer glared at Finn for a moment more, then turned away. "I can't believe you're doing this."

"It's not just me."

"The hell it isn't." Sawyer couldn't take discussing this for one more minute. He swiped his T-shirt off the floor and wrenched it over his head on his way out of the kitchen. He stopped at the front door. He didn't need to turn around to know Finn was behind him. He told him, "Enjoy the vacation."

There was a long pause. Then Finn whispered, "Don't go like this."

"Don't make me choose."

When he didn't get an answer, he yanked open the door and walked out.

* * * *

It was the longest two weeks of Sawyer's life. He did his job, stayed focused, completed the training drills, lifted weights, but he felt like he was just going through the motions. A part of him wasn't there.

Two weeks, and he hadn't talked to Finn once. He'd tried calling and texting, but Finn hadn't returned a single message. Which probably wasn't a bad thing. Sawyer still hadn't figured out what the hell to say to Finn to get him to change his mind.

When Finn got back to work on the Monday after his vacation, the team was suited up in full gear to attend an on-site field-training course with a woman from Homeland Security. Finn didn't acknowledge Sawyer, didn't even look his way as they stood not more than twenty feet apart, the rest of the SWAT team positioned between them, awaiting instructions in the abandoned building the department used for training.

The woman from Homeland entered the room. She was a tiny thing, but one look at her and he knew she was tough as hell and would take no shit from any of them. She was there to give them essential information that could help keep them and civilians alive, and they better listen up.

Her plan was to give an overview of three new recommendations on hostage situations during mass shootings, and then the team would go through the scenarios real-time in full tactical gear.

She asked for a volunteer to help with the demonstrations. Finn stepped up.

"You'll be a hostage." She took Finn aside and gave him some instructions, and then they returned to the group.

Standing beside Finn, she held on to him with one hand and pointed a semiautomatic handgun at his side as she said, "As we all know, when a gunman takes a hostage as a shield, there are several ways it can end. One being they'll use the hostage to commit suicide by cop."

Without warning, she shoved Finn away and aimed the weapon at him. "Bang." Finn went down.

He hit the ground flat on his back, like he'd really taken a bullet to the chest. The woman continued talking, but Sawyer didn't hear a word. His heartbeat pounded in his ears. He stared at Finn lying motionless on the ground, and in that moment everything was clear.

It hit him with immediacy and an intensity Sawyer couldn't have predicted despite all he'd seen in his career. How he would've felt that day had it been Finn who'd been shot, had it been Finn who desperately needed help to survive, all while Sawyer had to go on with the job, not knowing whether or not Finn was dying within his reach. The breath caught in his chest. "Jesus."

The commander turned to glare back at him. "What?"

Sawyer could barely find his voice. He forced the word out. "Nothing."

During the rest of the training, he did his best to focus on the woman from Homeland, on her demonstrations, and the training drills, all the while avoiding direct contact with Finn.

The man who'd been right about everything.

* * * *

Sawyer successfully avoided eye contact with Finn for the rest of their shift, but it was Finn who hightailed it to his truck after the post-training debriefing. Guess Sawyer wasn't the only one doing some avoiding.

Well, no more.

Which was why he found himself standing outside Finn's house, waiting for the smart son of a bitch to open the door and talk to him. He knocked again, but when he got no answer, he pulled out the key Finn had given him a while back and let himself inside.

He heard the shower running and headed down the hall toward the lone bathroom. He swung the door in but stopped short of stepping inside. Instead he leaned against the doorjamb and took in the sight of the bathroom. New paint color, new floor, new cabinet, new mirror, even the damn shower curtain was new. The realization that Finn had actually finished the bathroom, that he'd gone ahead with his plans without Sawyer there to help stung. Fiercely. Sawyer had worked with him on every other single thing Finn had done to the house since he'd bought the place.

It hurt worse to know that missing the bathroom redo was his own fault.

He watched Finn through a gap between the shower enclosure and the pale blue curtain. A naked, wet Finn. God, he was beautiful.

Finn was washing his hair, moving with agitation that kept the taut muscles of his shoulders and back and upper arms flexed. Even his ass and thighs were tense. He spun around to rinse his hair, bringing the front of his body into view. Rivulets of water ran down his chest, his abs, along the dark trail of hair leading south, then over his thigh muscles. Sawyer thought about the scar from the bullet wound on his own upper right thigh, a match to the one on his left shoulder, the two shots he'd taken that day he'd gone down during the raid on Pickett. He imagined what he'd feel if he were seeing those scars on Finn's body right then. He couldn't avoid the way that picture sat heavy on his chest.

Yet he couldn't help himself. He grinned because there was

also no way for him to avoid the very hard cock that was jutting out from Finn's body, bobbing with his sharp movements. Apparently being pissed-off got Finn all hot and bothered.

Sawyer made his way to the shower, kicking off his shoes and socks as he went, pulling off his T-shirt, then his jeans and underwear. He slid back the curtain and stepped inside.

Finn's eyes widened at the intrusion, but he said nothing.

Sawyer didn't hesitate. He approached and pressed his lips to Finn's. It was a sweet, chaste kiss unlike any they'd shared before.

Finn studied him with uncertainty. "What was that for?"

"You were right." Sawyer took a step back and leaned against the shower wall. "If…" He swallowed, drew in a deep breath, and forged on. "If it had been you in that house, if you had taken a bullet that day, I would've done anything to get to you, to make sure you were okay. I would've put everyone in jeopardy to save you."

Finn shook his head. "You'd never have done that. You'd have finished the job first. You'd give your life for any member of the team." With an uncharacteristic uncertainty to his expression, Finn bit his bottom lip. "But we can't pretend that this thing between us isn't going to affect our work."

"No, we can't. So…" Sawyer moved in closer. "Here's my answer." He ran the pad of his thumb over Finn's lower lip and the indentations left behind by his teeth. "I choose you. Us. Not the job." He repeated the action with his thumb. "Whatever it takes, we'll figure the rest out."

A quick breath passed through Finn's parted lips. "Are you sure?"

"I'm more than sure. You're not just one of the guys I work with anymore, and I can't keep pretending you don't mean everything to me."

When the last word left Sawyer's lips, Finn came at him, fast and hard, and had him flattened to the shower wall in a heartbeat. Sawyer returned the kiss with as much intensity as Finn was giving him.

The heated water ran down their bodies as they held on to each other, as they clutched and rocked and rode out the immeasurable intensity of the moment, one that was so different from any other they'd shared. All those days on the job together, all those nights in each other's bed, and Sawyer, not surprising considering his lack of experience, had not been prepared for the enormity of what he could feel for another person.

Amid the kissing, the grinding of wet body against body, they somehow managed to get the water cranked off and get themselves to the bedroom.

Sawyer shoved Finn down onto the bed. Without giving Finn a moment to catch his breath, he grabbed him by the hips and flipped him over. He advanced and got his tongue between Finn's ass cheeks, pouring everything he felt for the man into that one connection, loving on him in that most intimate of ways.

"Holy fuck!" Finn cried out as he tucked one leg under him to give Sawyer better access. "I love when you do that." He groaned, loud and long, and there was no better sound.

Sawyer loved hearing Finn whining and moaning, loved knowing it was him who was making that tough alpha male lose it. He quickened the swipe and swirl of his tongue, really going to town on Finn's ass.

Finn pounded the bed with a clenched fist, buried his face in the mattress, and groaned louder. "God, don't stop." His words were a muffled plea.

Sawyer shifted up so he was lying over Finn's body. He whispered in his ear, "I have to stop. So I can fuck you through the mattress."

"God, yes!" Finn reached behind him and gripped Sawyer's ass. "Now."

Sawyer chuckled. "Always so bossy." He lunged over Finn for the nightstand drawer. He got out the lube and sat up to slick his cock and Finn's ass. They had ditched the condoms long ago when it was clear they'd been fucking only each other for months. Things had gotten monogamous between them long before they had the nerve to admit it to each other. Dumbasses.

But what did it matter now? He had Finn right where he wanted him. He lay back down over Finn's outstretched body.

Finn looked back over his shoulder. "Kiss me."

Hell, yeah. It was sloppy, all tongue and wet lips, the slick sounds permeating the dimly lit bedroom, and it was just about damn perfect.

But Sawyer had to end it. "I'm gonna fucking bust a nut here."

Finn tucked his knee up higher under his body. "Do it." The lust in his low voice told Sawyer that Finn wanted this as badly as he did. Hell, Finn had been hard and wanting before Sawyer even got there.

Sawyer lined his cock up with Finn's ass. "Were you thinking about me doing this to you earlier in the shower?"

"Yes!"

With that one word, Sawyer drove forward. They both groaned in unison that time. He sank in farther and pulled back, wanting to drag this out but unsure if that was even an option. "I can't…"

"Don't."

He took Finn at his word and plunged into him without finesse. Over and over. Nothing—*nothing*—felt like that. The way Finn met his every thrust, head down, hands fisting the bedsheets, pressing his ass into Sawyer's movements with unbridled power and desire.

Sawyer jerked his hips faster, shoved into Finn harder. The headboard slammed against the wall with each drive forward. A new sound for Finn's bedroom. Either the bed had moved or there was a new level of intensity to their sex.

That thought spurred Sawyer on. He draped himself over Finn, loving the feel of heated flesh against flesh, the sound of skin slapping skin. He reached around with one hand and gripped Finn's shaft.

Finn groaned, and his fists tightened their hold on the sheets. "Yes. Sawyer."

Hearing his name in that low moan nearly did Sawyer in. He tried with everything he was to hold off his orgasm, determined to hear Finn lose it first. He stroked him faster, squeezing the head of Finn's cock with each pass, and Finn writhed under him, groaning loud as his release struck the sheets beneath them.

Sawyer kept on thrusting through the clench of Finn's ass, and his own orgasm crashed into him like roaring waves pounding the surf over and over again. He threw his head back and grunted at the ceiling.

When his body finally stilled, he collapsed onto Finn, and they both fell to the bed. The scent of sex and sweat permeated the air. Sawyer grinned, his lips pressed to Finn's shoulder blade.

They lay there for a long while, their bodies still connected, their rapid exhales the only sound between them. Sawyer didn't want to give up the contact, not yet.

Eventually, when he was afraid he was going to suffocate Finn, he shifted off and lay on his side facing him. A minute later when Finn turned his head to look at him, Sawyer asked, "So what do we do now?"

Finn sighed and rolled to his back. "Talk to the commander."

"Come clean?"

"Yeah."

Sawyer thought about that for a moment. It was the right call. Maybe Weston would have a suggestion on how they could get out of this fucked-up work situation they found themselves in. "Okay."

Finn looked shocked for a brief moment. Then he visibly relaxed. He raised his arms over his head and stretched. "Man, I could get used to this."

"To what?"

"You're not usually this…" He paused as if he was afraid admitting the next part would change something. "Affectionate."

It was only then Sawyer realized he'd been running his fingertips back and forth across Finn's chest. He kept it going for another minute, savoring the feel of Finn's body, loving on him in a completely new way. He couldn't keep away from him. It was that simple. He wanted to touch him, make him happy, offer him everything he had to give. With that thought, he let his fingertips sweep over Finn's chest hair for a moment

more. Then he sat up and slid closer so he was gazing down at
Finn. "You know, I'm older than you."

Finn's brows rose. "Man, I must be slacking if I've let you
forget that I know just how much older you are." He laughed.

Sawyer didn't. "I'm trying to be serious here. With the bullet
wound, my leg isn't exactly what it used to be." He struggled to
find the right words, then decided he just had to say it. "I think
it should be me."

"You?"

"Who transfers out of SWAT. I don't have that many years
left that they'll let me stay in tactical anyway."

"Right. You're not that old."

"Old enough. It should be me." Sawyer turned away and got
up. He went to the dresser and dug out two pairs of jeans. He
tossed one to Finn and slipped on the other pair. He stood
beside the bed, staring down at Finn. "I'll talk to the
commander tomorrow."

"No." Finn moved to sit on the other side of the bed and
yanked the pants on up to his thighs. "It's going to be me."

"Why?"

Finn hesitated for a moment, his head down. Then he stood,
tugged his jeans on the rest of the way, and faced Sawyer. "I
want it to be me."

"No way. You love the job."

"I did. For a long time. But… lately I've been feeling like
it's time to do something else." He gave a nod like the decision
was final. "I want to take the detective's exam."

Sawyer couldn't believe what he was hearing. He took a step
back, then paced the length of the room. "Why the hell didn't
you tell me this in the first place?"

"Because…" Finn shrugged as if he wasn't going to say
more. Then he added, "I wanted to know what I was giving up
SWAT for."

Sawyer stopped. His mouth fell open. "For us."

"For a man who I now know wants me more than anything."

He gaped at him some more. "You're fucked up."

Finn laughed. "Yeah. But before you said I was right about
the job, it seemed impossible to even think about quitting

SWAT. About leaving the guys, not working with you anymore. It's part of who I am. I guess, subconsciously at least, I wanted to know that it wasn't just me who'd make that sacrifice."

Sawyer snorted out a laugh. "I say again, you're fucked up."

Finn laughed with him. Then he dropped to the bed, sitting with his back to Sawyer.

Sawyer sighed and rounded the bed to sit beside him. "I'm having a hard time believing you."

"I'm telling you want I want. It's the right time for me to go. And it's not just because of us. I need a change."

"You should've told me."

"I know. I just wasn't sure until now. The shooting, and later when you were lying in the hospital, it all got me thinking. About us. About my future. About why I took the SWAT gig in the first place. I'm not the same twenty-five-year-old adrenaline junkie I was back then."

Sawyer snorted. "Are any of us?"

"No." Finn examined him with genuine contemplation. "But the job still suits you. Maybe in a way it never did me."

"That's bullshit. You were made for it."

"To be a cop? Yeah. The rest? I'm not sure anymore. I think I'm ready for something different."

Sawyer shook his head. Were they really talking about this? "Man, it always sucks when someone leaves the unit, but you..." He shook his head again. "This is going to change everything for me."

"And that's why I have to go."

"Yeah." He studied Finn. "You sure it's what you want?"

Finn held his gaze. "Yeah, I'm sure."

* * * *

Sawyer walked the length of Finn's front porch for what had to be the thirtieth time. He'd tried waiting inside, but he couldn't stand the silence of the empty house, so he'd headed back out and kept on pacing, kept on waiting.

Fifteen minutes later Finn's truck pulled up to the curb. The engine cut off, and Finn slipped out of the cab. He strolled up the front sidewalk, the relief evident in his gait, his posture, on his face. Which hit Sawyer like a brick. He hadn't had a clue how much all this had been affecting Finn until that moment.

"How'd it go?"

"Okay." Finn took the porch steps two at a time. He paused before Sawyer for a brief moment, and Sawyer couldn't read the expression on his face. Then Finn continued past him and on into the house.

Sawyer followed him in. Keeping quiet, he watched as Finn shrugged out of his coat and chucked his truck keys onto the hall table before heading into the living room and dropping down onto the couch with a loud sigh. "It was tough."

"I bet." Sawyer settled in beside him. "You sure this is what you want?" He had to ask again, had to hear it from Finn one more time.

"It is. It's just weird moving on." He met Sawyer's stare. "Telling someone about us."

"Did Weston freak out?"

"Nah. He said he figured a long time back that there was something going on, but if we didn't say anything and it didn't mess with our work, then it was none of his business."

"Sounds like him."

"I told him that it was starting to affect the job, and we needed to make a change."

"Was he cool about it?"

"Yeah. But I'm on desk duty until the transfer goes through. He said he wasn't taking chances with anyone's life."

Sawyer nodded. So this was it. No more call-outs together. God, this sucked. He looked to Finn again, and he knew... It would suck far more to give him up, to go back to just being friends. He stared off at the front door and thought about what it had been like waiting there earlier instead of riding home with Finn like usual. "We're not gonna see each other as much."

"Yeah." Finn picked at the fabric on the armrest of the couch like he was debating something, or searching for the right words.

"What?"

Finn shrugged. "Nothing."

"If even for a second you don't think this is what you want—"

"Stop." Finn flattened his hand on the arm of the sofa. He took one look at Sawyer, then leaned his head back to the couch behind him and grinned at the ceiling. A big-ass dopey grin like he'd just gotten the best damn news.

What the hell was he smiling at?

Then he started laughing.

"Want to let me in on the private joke?"

"Sure." He rolled his head Sawyer's way. "I just..." His expression grew thoughtful. "You love me."

"Oh." Relief washed over Sawyer. "Yeah, I do." It was getting easier to admit. To himself. To Finn. He reached for Finn's hand and slipped his fingers between the other man's. They sat there on the couch, their hands locked in that simple touch. They'd never done anything like that. Apparently it was the time for firsts.

They both continued to focus on their combined hands for a moment more. Then their eyes met. Instinctively Sawyer leaned in. The kiss started off sweet and sensual. Then everything shifted. Finn was clutching at the front of Sawyer's shirt, pulling him in closer, taking his mouth harder, and Sawyer gave back the same, cupping the back of Finn's head with one hand, running the other down the front of Finn's body.

God, he couldn't wait any longer. He shifted around to kneel before the couch as Finn spread his thighs and made room for him. Sawyer tugged on Finn's upper legs, pulling him toward the edge of the couch until he was close enough he could easily reach the opening of Finn's jeans. He popped open the top button, then started on the zipper, wanting him in his mouth so damn much he could already taste him.

Then Finn spoke in a low voice. "You could move in here."

Sawyer stopped with Finn's fly half-open. "Live together?"

"Yeah."

Could they really do that?

"Come on, Crenshaw." Finn nudged him with one leg. "We pretty much spend every night together anyway. And now there's no reason to keep up the pretense that we're just friends. That we need more than one bed." He winked at him.

"True." Sawyer pictured moving all his stuff into Finn's house, waking up next to him in bed, having breakfast together before they headed off to work. A pressure he hadn't realize was still bearing down on his chest lifted. "I've never lived with anyone before. I might suck at it."

"I'm pretty sure you will." Finn laughed. "We haven't killed each other yet. I think we'll figure it out." He slid his ass the rest of the way to the edge of the couch and tugged Sawyer forward at the same time so Sawyer was now bent over him.

"Yeah." Sawyer ran the pad of his thumb over Finn's lower lip. "We'll figure it out." He pressed a kiss to those delectable lips. "Together."

They sealed the deal with another drawn-out, tender kiss on the couch, and a hard fuck in Finn's bed—*their* bed now. That was just the way things had always been between them, a combination of friends and lovers, of mutual affection and smoldering heat that was too damn good to throw away, for any reason.

His Roommate's Secret

This story started off as a brief 460-word scenario titled "My Roommate's Surprise" and was originally shared via the author's website. It was later revised and expanded into the following novelette.

"Brady."

"Yeah?"

"I need to tell you something."

The hesitant sound of Rex's voice indicated that this was not going to be about the economics exam he'd been stressing over for the past week or whether I was planning to head to the gym later to lift weights.

Sitting at my desk in our dorm room, I closed the lid on my laptop and turned to face him. It was early morning, the rest of the world around us still quiet, no one playing pizza-box hockey down the hall or guys who were late for class thundering by our closed door.

Rex stood across the room in the open space between our beds, his strong body stiff and straight as he stared at the floor before him. "I'm gay."

Two words from my college roommate, and I couldn't blink, much less speak, or even keep my mouth from hanging open. I had to look like I was afflicted with some kind of spontaneous uncontrollable drooling problem.

I'd lived with Rex for the past two years, and I had no idea he was into guys. None.

Confusion rushed through me as I went over all the times I'd seen him head out on a date. How many of those nights were spent with men?

I thought we were the closest of friends, thought we'd pretty much covered the important shit about ourselves long ago. We'd spent a number of half-drunk nights during our first semester in the dorm shooting the shit about our pre-college lives, jobs we'd had that sucked, loves we'd lost, the worst sex of our lives, and the best.

I thought back on his "best" story. He'd described it as one long orgasm-filled weekend with an old high school friend he'd reunited with at a hometown wedding. The two of them alternated between fucking and something far more tender and passionate, something distinctly removed from his normal sex life and unlike anything he'd ever experienced before. I'd gotten turned on just listening to him talk about it, which had me feeling completely uncomfortable, what with my being a gay man getting all worked up over a hetero experience like that.

Had that story actually been about a guy?

I forced down a stiff swallow. "You're…"

"Gay." Rex's deep voice reverberated in the small room. That time he looked me in the eye as he said the word, speaking slowly as if I might not understand what he meant.

What a laugh. I'd known I played for the other team by the fifth grade, and apparently, not long after that, everyone in my life assumed the same thing. There was just something about me.

Rex, on the other hand, had always had a voracious appetite for women. And they for him. What with the tribal tattoos covering his upper body and a physique that had the female art students begging him to drop his pants for their Nude Drawings course.

He was the tough twenty-eight-year-old tattoo artist who impressed everyone when, on a dare from a customer in his shop, he filled out an application to OSU, and when he was accepted, decided to sell his business and stay in a dorm on campus so he could have the full "college experience."

Was this just about Rex wanting to do the college "curious

gay experiment" thing too? Or was he really telling me he already liked to fuck guys?

Which made no sense. He was always dating women. And fucking them.

Or so I'd thought.

Maybe I'd never really known him.

Maybe the past two years had all been an act.

Maybe all that daydreaming I'd done about waking up at night to find him in my bed, his body draped over mine, his lips on my dick, didn't have to be just a fantasy any longer. Maybe I could finally admit I was falling for him.

From where he stood across our room, Rex lifted his head and threw me his hallmark grin. The same smile that showcased the dimples, even through the dark stubble on his face. The one that also came with a pointed look in his eyes that said he was planning to tease me about my love of cock, which had been happening more and more often as of late.

I was beginning to get that I really had missed something about him. I got up from the desk and strode to the door of our room. I wasn't about to leave. I just needed to move, needed a minute to process what he was telling me. And what it might mean.

All those times I'd pushed aside my desire for him, all those moments I told myself not to lust after yet another straight guy... I stopped and turned to face him. "I thought you dated women."

"I do."

"You sleep with both?"

"Yes. Have since I was seventeen."

"So you're bi?"

He hesitated for a moment. "Technically, yes."

"Technically?"

"It's complicated."

I couldn't wrap my head around what he was trying to say. I studied him for a long moment, but he wouldn't look at me. "So un-complicate it for me."

He lifted his head and moved toward me, then halted suddenly, still halfway across the room. He held perfectly still and forced down a noticeable swallow like he had to keep himself from saying more. Or was finding it hard to stop himself from moving closer. "I have relationships with women. Not with men." He stopped talking again until I looked him in the eye. "I don't date guys. I fuck them."

"Oh." What did that mean? "So you fuck around with guys on the side?"

"No." He glared at me as if taken aback and completely offended by my words. "I've never cheated on anyone." The pointed stare continued. "Never."

I threw my arms up in an exaggerated gesture. "Sorry." I let my hands fall to my sides with a loud slap to my thighs. "I mean you say you're gay, but you're really bi. You say you don't date men, but you're telling me you screw them. It's a little confusing."

"I know. It's just…" He stopped again like he had to carefully plan out his next words. "When I'm single, I go out sometimes, pick up guys."

"Fuck them."

"Yes."

I gave him a long, hard look. "Why are you telling me this?"

Rex's expression softened. He scanned down the length of my body in a slow sweep, then back up, and finally met my stare. I'd gotten that look from guys before.

"Oh." Despite the space separating us, my breathing kicked up a notch. He wasn't much taller than I, but he was older, tougher, stronger, more masculine. All the things that had me drooling over him since day one. He had to know I wanted him that first week we'd started living together. I always figured he was just being polite and ignoring it. For both our sakes. "You wanna fuck me?"

His eyebrows rose in amusement. Or anticipation. I wasn't sure which.

"Yes," he said. Then, almost immediately, the light in his eyes fell away and was replaced by what looked like regret. The contradiction was jarring, to say the least.

He visibly gulped down another stiff swallow, closed his eyes, and shook his head. Seconds passed. He finally steadied his gaze on me once more. "Yes, I want to fuck you. But I just..." He started toward me again but paused after only two steps. He was watching me with an intensity I'd never seen from any guy before. It had all the desire I'd felt for him—and always tried to push aside—flooding through me in a rush. It was the most erotically charged moment of my life, and I wasn't even sure what he was trying to tell me.

"Brady..." Without more warning than that, he darted forward and wound a hand around the back of my neck. He sucked in a sharp breath like he'd been waiting for months to get his hands on me, like that touch alone had magnified his need to be with me. He watched me for a long moment. I wasn't sure what he was trying to see. "Can I kiss you?"

Was he for real? "Yes." The drawn-out plea didn't sound like me.

Apparently Rex didn't care. Or he liked that sound. He leaned in and drew me forward at the same time. His lips parted. Mine followed suit. Then he stopped, his mouth hovering over mine. His warm fingers dug into the back of my neck. Our combined loud breaths sounded harsh in the otherwise quiet room, each of us exhaling a rush of air onto the other's lips. I could feel how much he wanted this, wanted me. It was heady and powerful, knowing I had captivated him right then. Or maybe long before then. I wasn't sure. But I wasn't about to ask. Not at that moment.

Rex's gaze dropped to my lips. He licked his own, then moved in the rest of the way and pressed his mouth to mine.

The kiss started off slow, a soft brush of flesh. Then he stepped into it and deepened the meeting of our mouths. His tongue swept out and met mine. Immediately my entire body came alive, like I'd been sleepwalking through life before then. Nothing—*nothing*—had ever felt as explosive as that simple touch. I wrapped my arms around his neck and fed him all the pent-up longing I'd been hiding from him. I clutched at him, tugged him tighter to me. I couldn't get close enough. It felt the same for him.

We ground against each other, full body to body contact. The kiss went on and on, all primal need and consuming passion. The desperate way he held on to me, the way his mouth kept moving over mine, the rasp of his facial hair against my chin amid the power of that kiss, it all demonstrated how much he wanted this.

Without breaking the connection of our lips, he walked me backward. The backs of my thighs hit the wood surface of my desk, and he pushed me down to sit on the edge. He slid forward to stand between my legs, the outsides of his thighs sweeping along the insides of mine. Even with the two pairs of jeans between us, that contact sent a shiver down my body.

I couldn't stop my next response. I spread my legs wider to give him more access, and he moved in closer. I lifted my hips and worked my groin against him. He returned the action with as much vigor, thrusting against me with full force, moaning into my mouth. Holy fuck, I was going to come right there, barely touching any of his skin.

Then everything stopped. Rex pulled back. He didn't go far, though. He rested his forehead against mine. We were both panting, both hard and wanting. He let out a long exhale. "Brady."

"What?"

"I…" He shook his head. His thumbs caressed the sides of my neck as he spoke again. "Before this goes any further, I want you to know—" He stopped and drew in a deep breath like he desperately needed the extra air just to keep upright on two legs.

"What?" I asked again, searching his face.

"I want—"

The knock on the door was loud and brief. "Hey, jackass," came a voice through the closed door. "You coming or not?" It was Snyder. He lived in the room across the hall and had Intro to Film Studies with Rex. "Come on. Get your ass out here now, or we're gonna be late."

Rex turned to glare at the door like he was going to tell Snyder to fuck off, but instead he spoke to me in a soft reticent voice I hadn't heard from him before. "I have to go."

"Sure." Nice of him to start this conversation ten minutes before he had to leave for class.

He finally looked back at me. "We're taking a quiz."

"Yeah, okay."

Rather than head for the door, he kept his hands on me, his thumbs rubbing the sensitive skin of my neck again and again.

His stare never wavered, and his chest rapidly rose and fell with each breath. We had roughly the same color of brown eyes and dark hair, but with his eyes... I'd never seen anything so intense, even when he was laughing his ass off or smiling like a complete dork.

Another swipe of those thumbs. "Can we talk later?"

"Yeah," I said. "Sure, later." The words were barely audible, every part of me clenched in anticipation. Did he want to kiss me again? Did he want to bend me over the edge of my desk and sink into me? Did he prefer to get right to the fucking? Or would he take things slowly? Would he kiss and touch and pet more like we'd been doing for the past few minutes? Or was that an anomaly for him?

I ached to find out.

It was that simple. I wanted him. Hell, I loved him. So much it was hard to breathe somedays.

Rex licked his lower lip, and his eyes narrowed with delight, like he was tasting me on his mouth. "I'll see you later." He held still for a moment more, then dropped his arms and backed up a couple of steps, his eyes still zeroed in on mine. "Okay, later." With what looked like regret, he turned to leave, shutting the door behind him.

I gaped at that closed door of our room, in complete and utter shock at what had just happened.

Rex was into men. Tough, guarded tattoo-artist Rex who everyone fell for.

And he wanted me.

Me.

* * * *

I gave up on reading the notes from my Fundamentals of Engineering class, grabbed my coffee, and swallowed the last of it. I was practically vibrating with all the extra caffeine. I'd been sitting in the on-campus coffee shop for the past hour, not getting anywhere with my studying and not caring one damn bit.

When I had first walked inside the place earlier, I told myself I wasn't there just to wait for him. I had to study somewhere since our dorm was usually too loud at that time of day. Why not combine activities?

Only I wasn't getting any studying done. Still, I continued with the pretense, staring at my laptop screen. All I could see was Rex's face from earlier, the way he looked at me right before he kissed me. I couldn't get that heated expression out of my head. So for once since I'd met him, I let myself imagine everything we could have together. In his bed. In mine. On the floor. Against the closed door of our room because we couldn't wait to get our hands on each other. I hadn't thought about sex with one person that much since the crush I'd had on my American history teacher in high school.

With that thought, the front door of the coffee shop opened. I glanced up right as Rex entered. He didn't see me, just stepped up to the counter and ordered a coffee, which he didn't get in a to-go cup, so he was planning on staying. Like he did every Monday, Wednesday, and Friday between his afternoon classes.

As he turned away from the counter with his coffee in hand, he spotted me. I lifted my chin in a silent hello, and he returned the gesture, starting my way. He grabbed the back of the empty chair across from me, dropped his backpack to the floor, and sat, setting his coffee mug down before him. He didn't say anything at first, just studied me with that same intensity he'd been looking at me with earlier in our room. "Hey."

"Hey." I barely croaked the word out. I cleared my throat. There was something about the moment that felt like a date. A first date, all awkward glances and uncomfortable pauses, neither one of us knowing what to say next.

Or maybe that was just me. He smiled my way, his entire focus on my face. "Sorry I sprang all that on you this morning."

"It's okay. Why didn't you tell me before today?"

"I don't know. I never talk about it with anyone."

"It? That you're into guys?"

"Yeah, that, and other stuff. I just knew it was the right time with you."

"Why?"

Rex sat back sharply in the chair as if whatever spell he'd been under was suddenly gone. He took a swallow of his coffee, then returned the mug to the table but kept it clutched in his large hand. "I just couldn't ignore it any longer."

"Ignore what?"

He looked up at me in surprise. "You know what. You've known for a while now. You just didn't want to see it."

I had no idea what he was going on about.

He leaned forward and propped his elbows on the table, which gave the moment a more intimate feel, like it was just the two of us in that coffee shop. "I wasn't sure what would happen if I made a move. I didn't know if it was a good idea."

"Why not?"

He hesitated and glanced around the place. Was it the idea of saying more in public that bothered him? Or did he not want to say anything period? Or maybe it was something else entirely, because when he spoke again, it was with steady resolve. "I've never risked this much to be with anyone."

With each new piece of information, I was getting more and more confused. Risked what? Our friendship? People finding out about him? "What are you talking about? What would you be risking?"

His shocked reaction was immediate. I had said something wrong. Only I had no idea how I'd offended him. Or maybe I'd hurt him. That was if the falling expression on his face was anything to go by. Never in my life had I seen a hard-hitting guy like Rex look so... defeated, so broken. And I'd done that to him. I opened my mouth to speak.

"Brady," came a voice from behind me. I turned and found a girl from my computer programming class strolling toward us. "Thank you so much for e-mailing me those notes. You're a lifesaver."

I stood and gave her a nod. "No problem. Glad I could help out."

"You have no idea." She glimpsed Rex over my shoulder,

and as it went with everyone who looked his way, the breath momentarily caught in her throat. The second she recovered, though, she flashed him a smile.

Something unfurled inside me, a jealousy I'd never experienced before. One response ran through my mind: *Back off. He's mine.*

Was he?

Would he be if we slept together?

I held back the uncharacteristic possessiveness and chatted with my classmate for a moment more. She offered her thanks again and took off. I turned back to the table. Only… Rex was gone.

I scanned the coffee shop, but he was nowhere in sight. His backpack no longer sat beside his chair, and his nearly full coffee mug was still on the table before me. I dropped to my seat. He'd taken off.

What the hell was he doing? He wanted to fuck me, but he couldn't sit and talk to me for five minutes? Or tell me what was really going on with him? Apparently he'd decided to freak out about his admission, about that kiss, or he'd just plain changed his mind.

Or maybe it was however the hell I'd hurt his feelings.

Stunned and fuming, I crammed my laptop into my bag, stood, and headed for the exit. I shoved the door open and stepped into the cool spring air that still lingered after the rainstorm from the night before. I held still for a moment and let the chill in the air cool my heated body, if not my temper.

Maybe the two of us being more than friends was a fucked-up idea. Maybe just the thought of it was going to totally screw up our friendship.

Still. He couldn't just kiss me the way he'd done and then run from it.

Or maybe that was exactly what I should let him do.

We only had a month more of living together in the dorm. Neither one of us was planning to stay on campus after that. We'd talked about getting an off-campus apartment together for the next school year, but that wasn't set in stone. In a month, we could walk away from each other, and I'd never see him again.

"Fuck this." Maybe it was the fact that I'd now had a taste of him, but I couldn't let this go. I wanted answers.

I scanned the crowd around me on the sidewalk. Most of the people were students, likely on their way to class. I spotted Rex in the next block on the other side of the street near the Social Sciences building, moving at a quick clip in the opposite direction of our dorm. I gave chase.

I was out of breath when I finally reached him. I grabbed him by the arm and yanked him to a stop. "What the hell is wrong with you? Why'd you just leave like that?"

He kept on staring straight ahead. "Brady, just let it go."

"Let what go?"

"What happened today."

"How the hell am I supposed to do that?" I stepped around him and got in his face, waiting until he looked my way. "You kissed me."

He glanced around at the people moving past us.

"They don't give a fuck what we did," I snapped at him. "Or what we're going to do." I couldn't help but hint that I wanted more, a hell of a lot more.

"I know that." His jaw clenched with anger. *He* was pissed? Although his next words were spoken in a calmer, almost miserable tone. "It's not them I'm worried about."

"Then what is it?"

He looked right at me. "It's you." Then, without another word of explanation, he stalked off.

Me?

I rushed after him. He must've known I was trailing behind him. At the last possible second, he turned right and ducked into a side door of the Social Sciences building. I followed him inside, but by the time I was through the vestibule and had the inside door open, Rex was halfway down the empty narrow hall.

"Rex," I called out as I raced after him.

He kept on going.

"Goddammit, Rex. Please stop."

That time he did. He kept his back to me until I was at his side.

"Can't we talk about this?" When he didn't respond, I took that to be a positive sign. I glanced around and spotted an open classroom door down the hall. I tilted my head toward it. "Come on." Taking a chance, I led the way and breathed a sigh of relief when I heard him follow.

Once he stepped inside the empty room, I shut the door behind him and dropped my backpack onto the instructor's desk near the front of the room. He did the same, not even looking my way as he moved past me. The open room was set up for lectures, accommodating maybe fifty students, with rows of individual seats situated on built-in carpeted risers. Windows covered the far wall of the room next to the desks. Luckily the shades were drawn closed. I didn't want to have this discussion in front of the entire courtyard. Although one of the windows was still open a crack, letting in the chatter and shuffle of students rushing by. I ignored the world outside those four walls and went to him where he stood facing the risers, just staring off at row after row of empty seats, his solid arms folded across his chest.

He spoke without looking my way. "How many guys have you been with?"

The question startled me, had me feeling even more off-kilter. "What?"

"How many?"

"I don't know. I don't keep track."

He scoffed as if that had confirmed something for him.

"Why are you asking?"

"You don't share much about that part of your life. I've had to draw my own conclusions."

"And what did you come up with?"

He shook his head. "Forget it."

Hardly. Did he think I slept with everyone who came on to me? Or was he wondering if I was really gay? Which was worth a laugh. Although he'd never actually seen me with a guy, and it wasn't like I told him every time I hooked up with someone. Maybe he wanted proof. Wasn't that kiss back at our dorm room enough? Wasn't the way I felt about him obvious?

Or maybe there was another reason behind the question.

I thought about pushing him, forcing him to just come out and say what he really wanted to know, but then it hit me. Maybe talking wasn't the answer. I moved into his line of sight, studied his hard expression for a moment. Decision made, I leaned in.

He jerked back a step. "What are you doing?"

"What do you think?"

He had that broken, wounded look in his eyes again. "This isn't a good idea."

"Why?"

When he didn't respond, I moved into his space again, slower than before but with as much determination. He didn't stop me that time. If he really wanted to, he could lay me out with one punch.

I slipped my hands around his nape and tugged him forward. Our lips met, and at first Rex tensed under the touch. Maybe this was a very bad idea. Then all at once, he took possession of the moment, planting his hands at my waist and practically lifting me off the ground as he spun us around and backed me to the wall at the front of the classroom. He raised my hands over my head and held them there while he fed me the best damn kiss I'd ever had. His fingers slid between mine so he was holding my hands as he kept them pinned to the wall above my head. Something about the restraint of his hold, about giving myself over to him, felt liberating. I grasped his hands in return.

The kiss went on and on, Rex clutching my hands in his. When he finally pulled back, I sucked in a sharp breath as he dipped his head and kissed a path down my throat, then licked a line up the other side. He breathed deep as he swept his lips along my flesh, his stubble tickling my sensitive skin in a delicious way. "God, you smell so good." He nibbled up the outer edge of my ear and whispered, "I want you."

"Oh God." Rex taking me right there up against the wall in that empty classroom sounded hot as hell.

But then, with unexpected suddenness, he let go and backed away from me, shaking his head as he went, his gaze focused on the expanding stretch of floor between us.

The immediate loss of his strong hold, of his body against mine had my head spinning. "What's wrong?"

He wouldn't look at me. He raised two fingers to his mouth and ran them over his lower lip, his hand trembling. His breath came in short, ragged exhales. "I have to go."

"What? Why?"

He stood there like he was made of stone, like moving one more inch—forward or back—might just kill him. There was no denying how much he wanted to be with me. After all, he was the one who started all this that morning. Then why was he fighting it? I could think of only one reason.

"Rex, who hurt you?"

His jaw twitched as he clenched it shut. He kept his stare aimed at the floor. Finally he said, "I have to go." He was kind enough to meet my stare before he did. "I'll talk to you later."

"Sure." What could I say? Don't go? Beg him not to walk away until he talked to me? Not to go without plastering me to the wall and giving me another one of those spellbinding kisses?

Rex retrieved his bag and had the classroom door open and shut again in a flash, and he was gone. I stood there with my back against the wall and stared out at all those empty seats, wondering how many times I could take watching him walk away from me after having him in my arms like that.

* * * *

Seven hours later I sat alone in our dorm room, still confused as hell, sick at the thought that this might be the end of things between us, the end of our friendship and any chance of more. I hadn't seen one sign of Rex since the classroom in the Social Sciences building, and I was getting angrier by the hour. I glanced at the clock beside my bed. It was after ten p.m. His classes were done at five.

We sometimes did our own thing on Friday nights, but he never just took off right after class, not even dropping off his backpack before heading out. And tonight we were supposed to go to a party at an off-campus house with a group of guys from our dorm.

A knock sounded on the door. Speaking of which… I closed the lid on my laptop, got up, and grabbed my coat. I turned off the overhead lights as I swung open the door.

Snyder stood in the hall with his roommate and three other guys. "You ready?"

Was I? I glanced back into the dark room behind me.

"Come on," Snyder said. "Don't even think of saying you have to study."

"No, I'm coming." As I closed the door to our room, I tried to tell myself I was only going because I had promised I'd hit this party with the guys, and I hated when friends bailed on each other like that, not that it had anything to do with avoiding Rex.

Right.

Snyder was watching me out of the corner of his eye as if he knew something was up. "Rex said he'd meet us there."

I jerked to a stop in the middle of the hall. The other guys kept on going for the staircase, but Snyder paused beside me.

"You talked to him?"

"He texted me an hour ago."

"Where's he at?"

"I don't know. Just said he'd see us there later. Everything okay between you two?"

"Sure. Why wouldn't it be?" I brushed it off with a shrug. "Everything's fine." Was it? Rex was coming to the party. Did I even want to see him at that point?

Yeah, I did. So much more than I wanted to admit, even to myself. I desperately needed to understand what he'd been trying to say earlier. I needed to find out why he kept walking out when things were just getting good between us.

And no matter what, I needed to tell him what I was feeling for him, what I had been feeling for a long time.

* * * *

The crowd was getting more drunk and horny by the hour. I was tired of nameless girls coming up to me and not saying much of anything before they were all over me. Most of them had to know I was gay, but they still gave it a try, probably hoping I swung both ways.

It was after midnight, and Rex was nowhere in sight. Apparently he was going for a degree in avoidance. The part of me that had been pissed off since our classroom encounter was now taking the reins.

I ducked out of the action on the first floor as soon as I could manage and headed upstairs. Almost all the doors to the bedrooms were closed, and as I walked by I could hear the low groans, the wet kisses, the squeak of the mattresses. At least a few of my fellow classmates were having a good time.

I leaned against the wall beside the only open door, debating whether I should step inside and lock the door behind me, fake myself a hookup to avoid having to go back downstairs.

I was being a coward hiding up there. I knew it, but I didn't give a fuck. I wasn't sure if I could handle facing Rex just yet. I was still trying to work through what I'd say to him.

I dropped my head forward and stared at the dingy hallway carpeting. How many college students had trudged over that carpet during the past year? Which got me wondering... How many guys had Rex been with since we'd started school almost two years earlier? And all the while I'd had no idea.

My eyes fell shut, and I was back in our room that morning, back to that moment he told me he wanted to fuck me, to that earth-shattering kiss. I mentally ran through the same sexual scenarios as I had in the coffee shop earlier. Only this time, every moment with Rex was more intense, more intimate. We were naked and on his bed, and he was kissing me again, touching me everywhere, worshipping my body. It was everything I wanted with him.

I breathed deep as I pictured him leaning over me, licking his bottom lip like he'd done in our room that morning before he'd left, then dipping his head down and taking my cock between his wet, warm lips. Had he ever sucked a guy off? Or did he just fuck? I'd been with a couple of guys who claimed to be straight but wanted my ass anyway. Only, that's all they wanted. No other touching, no sucking. What was Rex like in bed with men?

I wanted more than anything to find out.

Footsteps sounded on the stairs. "Brady, you up here?"

I jerked my head up and forced my thoughts out of the fantasy. "Yeah."

Rex bounded up the last of the stairs and then headed down the hall toward me. "Hey. I was looking all over for you." He wore a fitted black T-shirt over his broad chest. The sleeves of the shirt were tight and short, showing off his ripped upper arms that were covered in those black tribal tattoos. He also had on a pair of jeans that showcased the impressive thighs and the heavy bulge hidden under the zipper. I couldn't decide where I wanted to put my hands more.

I shrugged. "That fucking music was giving me a headache." The beat from the party below was still pouring up the stairs, and it was a perfect match to the quickening of my heartbeat as Rex moved in closer.

He propped himself against the wall beside me so we were standing shoulder to shoulder, not touching but so close I could feel the heat of his body. He threw me a sheepish grin. "Sorry I bailed on you earlier." He tipped his head back to the wall behind him and sighed heavily.

"I get it. You regret what happened. No big deal."

He snapped his head my way. "God, no. That's not it." With a confidence I didn't expect to see from him in that moment, he moved to stand before me. "I just don't want anything to mess up our friendship."

"Who says anything will?"

He seemed surprised by that. The corners of his lips turned up in a grin. The smile lingered for a few seconds more before he grew serious again. "I just couldn't take it if I lost you."

With those words, hope thundered through me that this might be about more for him than merely getting me into his bed.

Slowly, deliberately he leaned in until his lips hovered over my ear. "I want to touch you again. I want to do everything we didn't get to in that classroom."

I sucked in a quick breath. He smelled of the cologne he always wore, rich and woodsy, with a hint of something tropical, like standing on an ocean beach, only I'd never been this close to that scent. I whispered in return, "Nothing's stopping you."

He drew back and considered me for a long moment. He looked uncertain, like he was trying to figure out what I was really telling him with those words. Hell, I was too.

"Do you mean that?" he asked.

"Yeah."

"What if I told you I want more than just this one moment? A lot more."

I closed my eyes and relished those words. "Don't say that unless you mean it."

He didn't respond. I opened my eyes. With a sharp and unexpected abruptness, he backed up to the hallway railing overlooking the stairs. He spun to face the staircase, clutching the railing in both hands, his knuckles turning white with the grip. I just stared at his back and waited.

A few seconds later, he finally let go and ran his hands through his dark hair, the tattoos on both upper arms flexing with the movement of those tense, taut muscles. He whirled to face me. There was something in those penetrating eyes I'd never seen from him. Anticipation? Hunger? "So you want me?"

Was he serious? "No," I said as sarcastically as I could manage. "I'm just standing here with my dick hard enough to bust through my jeans. But I don't want you." I rolled my eyes. "You're a moron."

I thought my response might piss him off. Apparently not. He folded his arms across his chest and grinned at me again. Maybe he'd meant "want me" in a different way. He said, "I'm starting to get that I've been pretty stupid for a while now. But…" He lowered his gaze until the scuzzy carpet seemed to completely fascinate him. It was his next words that captivated me. "I don't want to be just another notch on your bedpost."

"What?"

He met my stare. "Do you ever fuck anybody twice?" His voice had taken on a harsh, bitter tone.

"I have, yeah," I bit back. Once or twice. Not that I got laid all that often. And not with anyone I was really into. Most of the time it was about scratching an itch. I hadn't found a guy yet who'd meant anything to me. Not the way he did. "What does it matter who or how many I've been with?"

"It matters." He moved farther into my space. "Because I haven't known you to spend more than an hour or two with anyone. In or out of bed." His voice rose with each word. Thank God for the music still pounding away downstairs.

"So," I said. "Big deal. Most of the guys I hook up with aren't the type I want to spend my downtime hanging with."

"Yeah?"

"Yeah. I'd rather spend that time with you."

We held the stare, and the air between us seemed to change, grew heavier in an instant. His eyes narrowed with the same look of lust he'd given me in our room earlier. He took another step forward.

A door down the hall flung open, and Snyder came barreling out of the room with his arms wrapped around his girlfriend's waist. She was giggling and tripping over her feet. Snyder gave a nod our way and steered her down the stairs without a word to us.

Rex and I were standing close. Too close. What would Snyder think? What would Rex? Did he want people to see us together? To know about him?

When Snyder and his girl were gone, Rex turned to me again and studied my face. He must've seen something he liked. "Come here." He gripped me by the hips and yanked me away from the wall. He backed me into the open bedroom, kicking the door shut behind us, then crowded me farther inside before he let go of me.

The room was dark, but the moon outside was bright and high and shone through the thin curtains enough that there was no missing the bed beside us or the fact that it was Rex that I was about to get horizontal with.

I waited for him to come to me the way he'd done in our room that morning, but he didn't.

That fear in his eyes that I'd seen in the coffee shop earlier was back. I couldn't help myself. I moved in and clasped him by the forearms. "What's wrong? What aren't you telling me?"

He took a step out of my reach. Then another. He kept going until he was at the door of the room. He leaned against it. His head fell back to the wood surface. I didn't know if I should try to go to him again or give him space. No missing the irony of that. Because for once in my life, I didn't want to run from an emotional moment. I didn't want to take off on someone before things could even hint at getting serious. This was Rex, and I wanted to know what was wrong with him, wanted to help him, even if I never got to be with him.

I was still wavering over my next move when Rex started to speak, his voice tight with emotion, his head still tilted back against the door. "When I was a senior in high school, I fell for a guy. I met him at a gay bar I'd been going to for a few weeks. He was a couple of years older, had his own tattoo business, an apartment. I was young, and he was more experienced, and I fell hard." He seemed to struggle to swallow, to go on with the story. "I kept on seeing him until I graduated. Then we moved in together, and I started working at his shop." Rex paused again and let out a ragged sigh. "I lived with him for five years before I found out he'd been cheating on me the entire time."

"Shit."

"Yeah. I guess he didn't see us the same way I did. One night I spotted him getting blown by a guy behind our apartment building. I confronted him. He said he loved me, but he could never be with just one man, that it wasn't in his nature. He thought I got that. I felt so completely stupid. I thought he had just wanted me that entire time. I thought we were happy. Committed."

"Asshole."

"Yeah." He stopped like he was considering that. Or maybe something else, maybe looking back on those days from a more detached perspective. "I thought I had this perfect life. A fantastic guy, great apartment, a job I loved. In one moment I lost it all."

Everything was starting to make sense. "And after that, you stopped dating men."

Keeping his head against the door, his gaze on the ceiling above, he nodded. "I guess I figured women could commit more easily." He laughed as if that was the biggest joke in the world. I didn't get the punch line. Maybe it had something to do with the fact that he'd never been in a long-term relationship with a woman.

"Why didn't you ever tell me this?"

"I never tell anyone. I didn't think it mattered."

"And now it does?"

He nodded again.

I thought back on his words about women and commitment, about the relationships he'd mentioned whenever we talked about our pasts. "You've never really gotten that serious with anyone since then. Or have you?"

"No. Never found someone who meant enough to go there with." He finally dropped his head and looked my way. "Until now."

The breath caught in my throat. "Are you saying what I think you're saying?"

"You need me to spell it out?"

"Yeah, I think so."

A heartbeat passed. Another. Then Rex crossed the room. He had his body against mine, his arms around me in a flash. He spoke without words, kissing me again, slower than at the dorm, taking time with each soft sweep of his lips and his tongue against mine, really exploring that simple caress of two mouths. He had his hands splayed across my back, holding me to him.

I grabbed him by the hips and tugged him closer, needing to feel all of him against me. He moaned into the kiss, and that had one specific part of me aching for him in no time. He must've noticed my body's reaction to the proximity of his. He moaned again, then kissed me again.

He didn't tease or hesitate that time. Instead he held me by the nape and kept on going with the kiss, pouring what felt like more than two years of longing into it, into each touch of his lips to mine, each swipe of his tongue. In no time the kiss became passionate, wild, and it ended with me panting, sprawled out on my back across the bed, his body pressing into mine in all the right places.

He pulled back and threw me a grin as he rubbed my cock

through my jeans. "Do you know how long I've waited for this?"

I wanted to ask exactly how long, but before I could speak, he got the zipper down on my jeans, the opening parted. He worked his hand inside and gripped my erection. With the feel of his palm against my heated shaft, I gasped and arched into him. "Shit, Rex. I…"

"Yeah?" He moved his hand along my length, slowly, torturing me with the lightest of touches. "You what?" Another slow stroke, and then he tightened his grip and picked up speed. "Tell me."

I couldn't keep still. I shifted my hips forward and back. I groaned loud and long. "Fuck, I've waited so long for this too."

With sudden determination he let go of me, pulled me up and off the bed with him. He spun us around, and then he sat on the edge of the mattress. He tugged me to him so I stood between his legs as he peered up at me with a vulnerability I'd never seen from any man before. "How long?"

"What? That I've wanted you?"

"Yeah."

"Since the first time you walked into our dorm room."

His eyelids lowered for a brief moment as he exhaled a long breath. Then he was all action again. He grabbed my jeans in both hands and yanked them down to my knees, his eyes completely focused on mine once more. He cupped my cock through my briefs, stroking my length. Without removing my underwear, he leaned forward and took the tip of my dick between his lips. He sucked hard, wetting the fabric of my underwear and the head of my erection, swirling his tongue around and around and pressing at the slit. It all felt amazing, had my head spinning, and my goddamn briefs were still in the way. What the hell was it going to be like without anything between us?

As if he could hear my thoughts, he lowered my underwear, taking his mouth off me for the briefest of moments before capturing my cock in that wet heat again, this time his lips and tongue making contact with my skin.

I groaned. "God, yes."

He never let up. His hands were on me now, cupping my balls and jerking the base of my dick as his mouth raced along the top half. Looking down at him, seeing his head bob over me like that was intoxicating. Forget the beer. This was enough of a high to last all damn night.

He sat up taller and plunged that delicious mouth all the way down my length in one motion, holding tight with those wet lips as he made his way back up to the tip. He repeated the action again. And again. I cupped the back of his head, digging my fingers through his short hair. My legs began to shake. My ass clenched. I whimpered. "I'm gonna come."

He stopped. "Not yet." He stared up at me, his lips wet with his own spit and the evidence of my arousal, and in that moment I knew what he wanted.

I nodded. I stripped my jeans off the rest of the way, shed my shirt as he did the same with his clothes. When he sat on the bed again, I took a moment to admire the sight before me, all that bare, sleek flesh over hard muscles. He really was an amazing-looking man.

And he was about to me mine.

I straddled his strong thighs and kissed him again, pressing my weight into him until we were lying on the bed. God, that solid body under mine felt incredible.

We were both ready to go off, especially once we were finally naked and on the bed tangled up together. We kissed, rolled, thrust against each other, and a short moment later—far too short—I felt the familiar pull.

He maneuvered us around so he was on top again and stared down at me. "Fuck, this is…"

"What?"

He shook his head as if saying more right then was too much. He lined us up so our cocks met, and he began moving again, rubbing our erections together between the slide of our bodies. I groaned. I was close. "Shit."

He didn't let up. He rocked faster, bringing himself along with me. His breaths grew rapid, ragged in my ear. He grunted as he worked us together in an explosive rhythm, and that was it. I was done for. I threw my head back, arched against him, and it was explosive, crashing, as if every cell in my body was vibrating with the orgasm.

He kept on humping against me again and again, like nothing could stop him. Then he followed me into that sweet release. He let out a low moan, his face buried in the side of my neck, one hand clasping my upper arm, the other fisted in the blanket beneath us as his hips jerked through the shudders of his climax. Draped over me, he had his mouth latched on to the sensitive skin of my neck as the final spasms of pleasure shook his body.

When we were both still and breathing even again, he slid off and dropped to his back on the bed beside me with a loud sigh. "Damn."

"Yeah." I rolled to face him. In the dim moonlight, with his eyes closed, his head tipped back, he reminded me of a gladiator after battle, all sweaty and flushed and high on the triumph. I let myself have a long look, basking in the thought that it was me who had given him that expression of blissed-out ecstasy.

I wanted us to stay like that for another hour or two. But I had to know.

As soon as his eyes opened, I asked, "Now what?"

He didn't date men. He fucked them. All because some asshole had broken his heart.

Did that mean he was done with me? Was that why he was so worried this would mess up our friendship?

Rex kept on staring at the dark ceiling. So long I feared his answer.

No, scratch that. I was terrified.

Then a slow, amused grin formed on his lips. "We fuck our way through finals."

A nervous laugh surged out of me. "Yeah?"

"Oh, yeah." He turned to his side so we were lying face-to-face. "Did you mean what you said?"

"About what?"

"That you haven't been serious with anyone because it wasn't the right guy?"

"Yeah."

"Do you think you've found him now?"

His words were nearly my undoing. What was he saying? Was I that for him? He wouldn't be cruel and hint at that if he didn't mean it. Would he? Not on purpose. I said what I needed to say, really the only thing I could say. "Yeah, I have."

He smiled at me with sudden and resounding relief. He gave me a long, slow kiss, then shifted to lie on his back again. "Well then, I say we get that apartment we talked about, as soon as the semester ends instead of waiting for the fall. You could skip going home this summer, find a job here in town. We'll get a one-bedroom with a big bed for two."

"You want to live together? Like that?"

He moved to lean over me again, a stunned look on his face. "You don't?"

"Yeah, I do. I just..." What the hell could I say? "I wasn't sure what you wanted past this." I indicated the bed, the room around us.

"You thought this was just about getting at your dick?"

"I don't know. You were being cryptic as hell." I laughed again, more of that nervous sound escaping me like a balloon losing air. It was the tension of the longest day of my life draining away. But I needed to be sure. My heart was on the line here. Something I'd never risked before. "What was this for you?"

He laughed that time. So long and loud I thought I might slug him just to stop that sound and get him to answer me. His eyes were alight with what looked like adoration as he scanned my face. "I thought I was being so obvious." He studied me for a few more seconds, the big-ass grin still locked on his face. "Maybe it's different with guys."

"What is?"

"Showing them what they mean to you." He shook his head. "I always figured it was women who needed to hear the actual words." He came forward. "Brady." He paused as if to emphasize his next point. "I'm completely in love with you."

"Oh." I lay there, staring up at him with my mouth hanging open, just the way I'd been earlier that day when he'd told me he was gay. "You love me?"

"Yeah. Have for a while now."

"So this isn't just sex for you?"

"No. Which is kinda why I was freaked." He continued to look into my eyes. "Why I was afraid. I didn't know if I could risk losing you, risk you taking off on me. Risk falling for someone who might not want me the way I did him."

"Not want you?" He didn't get it. "Rex, I fell for you the first week I met you. I haven't been serious with anyone because they weren't you. So you can relax, because I don't want anyone else. And I'm not going anywhere."

He let out a long breath, and that time the grin reached his eyes in an entirely new way. As if he couldn't contain the emotion and needed something else to focus on, he glanced around the room and let out a nervous laugh. "I'm thinking we'll need to move at some point, though. This isn't exactly our room."

"Sure. But not yet." I pulled him to me. "I'm not nearly done with you yet tonight."

That time the sex was slower, tender in a way I'd never been with anyone. And as we lay there afterward, catching our breaths, he said, "I have a new best sex story now."

I thought back on the way he'd described that weekend with his old friend. I turned and buried the smile in his shoulder, then kissed his bare skin. "Me too."

He wrapped his arms around me, and I settled into the embrace, comfortable with him in a way I'd never been before. He wasn't just my roommate any longer. He was my friend, my lover, my everything.

Swept Away

"Motion denied."

I tried not to flinch, but the judge's decision hit me hard.

"Your Honor—"

She gave me a stern look that said don't push it, and I backed off. I've been told I'm a dominating presence in the courtroom. I wasn't sure what it was about me. Maybe the tats across the back of my fingers didn't convey I was a by-the-procedures kind of guy, although that's exactly what I was.

This was my first time in her courtroom, and I couldn't afford to push my luck on a long shot. Not this early in the game. The Ohio LGBT Coalition for Equality needed this win and part of that was not pissing off the judge.

"Thank you, Your Honor." I took a seat in the solid wood chair, and I just knew my underwear would be stuck to my ass when I stood again. The courtroom wasn't nearly as hot and humid as the heat wave outside, but with the air conditioning on the fritz it was unbearable, to say the least. I could feel the sweat streaming down my back, soaking a line down the dress shirt I had on under my jacket. My tie felt like it was trying to strangle me. I couldn't wait to get home and strip down to nothing.

I resisted the urge to rub my temples. Not like that would help anyway. Nothing eased the ache that had been pounding in my head on and off for months. Since the president of the Coalition had taken a seat in my office (back when five inches of snow had been on the ground) and had told me about the elderly gay couple who'd been forced into separate rooms when they'd moved from their senior community apartment to the on-site assisted living facility.

This was the case I'd become a lawyer to win, and the stress was taking its toll.

The judge spoke again as she dabbed at her upper lip with a tissue. She looked miserable. The heavy robe had to be worse than my suit and tie. The industrial fans they'd brought into the courtroom didn't do much to help. They just blew the humid air and the scent of everyone's sweat around the room. They also left me straining to hear the judge, which was doing nothing for my headache.

"Very well," she said. "If there's nothing further, Counsel, I will see you both Wednesday morning at eight a.m." She adjourned the court and was off like a shot for her private chambers. Maybe she had a secret window AC unit and was also going to strip down to nothing and stand in front of the window. Maybe I could hire some kid to climb the fire escape on the building next door and take pictures to blackmail a win in the case. I almost laughed at that, but I was too damn hot to muster the energy for even a half-ass chuckle.

I slipped the paperwork for the filed motion into my backpack, said goodbye to the representative from the Coalition, and left the courtroom. I was dying to get home and into a cold shower. The hallway outside the courtroom was even worse than inside had been. Apparently circulated, rank, humid air was better than nothing. I picked up the pace and headed for the elevators. I wanted to get out of there before the press or anyone else could stop me. After the shower, I was parking my naked ass on the couch in front of a fan, kicking back with a cold beer and a mindless action flick or two, and I wasn't moving until the morning.

"Hey, Eddie. Wait up."

Damn. Ten feet from my escape route.

I sighed and faced Tony. I'd known him for years, and it wasn't his fault I was tired and in a shitty-ass mood. In fact, I always felt like I owed the guy something. Maybe that's why we'd stayed friendly all these years. It had been his ass I'd been chasing when I conned my way into that private party in the normally-hetero sports bar fifteen years earlier. I hadn't known then it had been Tony's private party—with a few dozen of his closest gay friends in attendance—or that the tough bald guy named Mike working behind the bar would rock my world. I'd just been after a blow from the lawyer with the pretty lips.

Tony was out of breath when he reached me. "Damn heat." He wiped his brow with the back of his hand. "I heard about the judge's ruling. Sorry it didn't go as you'd hoped."

"Thanks. It was worth a shot."

"Definitely." Tony knew about risks. He took them all the time. It was what made him one of the top civil rights attorneys in the state. A slew of high-profile clients paid him a shit-load of money to "fight the good fight" as he always called it. He could afford to host all the private gay orgies he wanted, while I took on neighborhood nuisance gigs, representing the little guy for a minor fee. Hell, if I didn't win this case I might not even be doing that any longer. The president of the Ohio LGBT Coalition for Equality said they had hired me because they wanted someone hungry for a big win. She'd come to the right person, then. I was starving for it.

Tony slapped me on the shoulder and let his hand linger a moment too long for a couple of colleagues standing in the hallway of the courthouse. He always did stuff like that. He was a big guy, but at several inches shy of six-foot, he liked to assert his strength and dominance as often as he could. Or maybe he just liked touching me. Mike had told me plenty of times over the years that Tony still had a thing for me. Maybe I should have let him blow me that night fifteen years ago. Maybe that would've gotten me out of his system. But ten minutes inside that bar, and I'd had my sights fixated on someone else. Little did I know the next day I'd be heading into my first long-term relationship—a monogamous relationship, at that.

Not that I'd go back and do anything differently. Even if it meant Tony would stop groping me in the courthouse. From day one, Mike was it for me.

Tony gave a last squeeze to my shoulder and asked, "You and Mike ready for tomorrow night?"

"Yep. Fifteen years deserves something." Not that we were

planning anything special. We'd done the same thing every year, and I wasn't all that excited about our usual plans this time around. I was proud of us for making it this far as a couple, though.

"Hell yeah," Tony said. "I'm looking forward to seeing the whole gang. I'll catch you at the bar around ten." He was backing down the hall the way he'd come.

I nodded and took off for the elevators again. My head was pounding more than before talking to Tony. I just wanted to get my ass to my air conditioned car and then home.

The elevator doors opened and a blast of warm air hit my face. Great. Maybe the city would get the AC working over the weekend and this would be my last ride in the elevator from hell.

My phone vibrated in my pocket. I fished it out and checked the display as I stepped into the elevator. It was Mike. I hit the answer button and heard the roar of music and laughter from the bar before the phone was at my ear. Mike still owned the same place where we'd met. I called it his "other man." His other love, to be more precise.

"Hey. You busy already?" I asked. Apparently happy hour started early for some. Later for struggling civil rights attorneys. Or maybe never. It wasn't like I would describe myself as happy these past few weeks, even with a few drinks in me. Stress is called a silent killer for a reason.

"Eddie? I can barely hear you." He was shouting into the phone, so I heard him just fine.

"Go into the storeroom." I said the words louder than my elevator-ride-from-hell companions preferred if their looks were anything to go by. Apparently a heat wave this early in the summer pissed everyone off until we were all a bunch of grumps trudging through our days.

Mike must have taken my advice, whether he heard me or not. The background sounds of the bar muffled in my ear. "That's better," he said. "How'd it go today?"

"As I expected. The motion was denied. Opening statements on Wednesday."

"Damn. I'm sorry."

"It's okay. It's not like I wasn't prepared for it."

"Still sucks." He paused for a moment, and I could picture the expression on his face going from that concentrated frown to his I-want-your-ass leer. Maybe I'd heard an exhale or something. Or maybe I just knew him so damn well I didn't need to see his face to know what he was going to say next. "Tomorrow night I'll help you forget all about it. Me, you, a little celebration."

And forty of our closest friends. Hell, a few strangers too.

Every year on our anniversary Mike threw a private party at the bar to celebrate. A way to relive the night we'd met. The same bar and the same crowd of guys (looking a little older with each year), bringing along whatever guy they were into at the time.

I'd wear my leather pants and vest with nothing underneath, just like the first time, showing off the tats that spanned the length of my arms. Mike was fairer skinned than I, and he loved my darker complexion and the look of my skin against the black leather. He also loved my art, but every year at our anniversary party he was downright obsessed with the tattoos. He'd trace them with his fingers, his lips, kiss and lick them all night long. Maybe he'd been staking his claim, showing all our friends, acquaintances, and those few strangers that I was his. Which made sense with how the rest of the night always went. Because at some point we ended up fucking. Not in his office or in the storeroom. Right out in the bar in front of everyone. Sometimes he'd bend me over a table in the corner. Sometimes he'd blow me on the dance floor. No matter where or when, everyone would stop what they were doing and watch us, cheer us on. We were the live show they'd been waiting for all night.

It was hot as hell in the beginning. Like that first night. Once I'd gotten a look at him, I sat at the bar and had a few drinks, talking shit with him as he worked. Then he'd asked me to join him on the other side, and without another word, he'd spun me around and fucked me up against the bar while I faced the sea of men. I couldn't even remember his name once his dick was inside me, but I knew I wanted to see him again.

And every year after, we relived that moment. The bar. The booze. The crowd of men. The public fucking.

God, I was sick of it. But I didn't want to say anything to disappoint him on his favorite night of the year.

We weren't in the scene much anymore, and his bar was normally as hetero as the average population. That one night meant a lot to him, took him back to his younger days, to the leather bars, the excitement of casual, got-to-have-it now sex, the thrill of meeting me. He always said the best part was remembering the moment he first saw me, the moment he'd found something special he hadn't even known he'd been aching for.

"Eddie, you there?" he asked over the phone, bringing me back to our conversation.

"Yeah."

The elevator doors opened, and I made my way through the courthouse lobby and outside. The humidity level rose with each step I took toward the parking garage. I didn't bother ditching the suit jacket. What was the point now? My shirt had to be soaked underneath. I'd strip as soon as I got in the front door of our place, and maybe I'd just burn the damn suit when I was done with my shower.

"God babe, I've missed you lately." His voice had taken on that low rumble that matched the leer I'd been picturing. "I'm really looking forward to tomorrow night."

"Me too," I said. That was partially true. I missed him something fierce. Missed the way we'd been six months earlier. Before I'd taken this case. Before he'd made the decision to expand the bar and add on a restaurant. Before we'd both started working all hours of the day and night.

I was so damn tired I doubted I'd even get it up at the party. Nothing like forty guys staring at you, waiting for your dick to get hard. Once upon a time that had been a thrill. Now, I just wondered if they were all going to judge my technique, or lack thereof.

I used to worship Mike's cock through the longest blowjobs I'd ever given, teasing and sucking for all I was worth, easing off whenever he got close, until he was begging me to let him come. I hadn't done that in a long time. It all just seemed like too much effort. Most days we were too exhausted to do more than get off quick and hit the sack. Hell, I hadn't even blown him in two months. We were pretty much jerking off together in the shower or in bed before we'd both collapse for a few hours sleep.

I wanted those jaw-exhausting blowjobs back. I wanted him to be so hot for me he couldn't wait till I got undressed to have me, maybe even taking me up against his bar after closing. Just not with the live audience watching us.

"Listen," he said. "I gotta go. The contractor's meeting me in a few. That was the other reason I called. Could you pick up Steven at the airport? I can't get away from here for a couple more hours."

Steven. So much for spending the night naked on my couch with a cold beer. I could probably still go for the beer, but no way in hell was I sitting around with my balls hanging out while Steven—Mike's ex—stared at me.

They had remained friends from the day they'd broken up, even though Steven now lived in New York. He'd been at the bar the night I'd met Mike, and every year he flew back to attend our anniversary gig. Some traditions really needed to die a miserable death. Not that Steven was a bad guy, just one more reason in a long list why I was finding our usual thing tiresome.

"What time?" I asked.

"His plane lands in half an hour."

So much for getting out of the suit. And the cold shower. "All right. I'll take care of it."

"Great. I told him I'd meet him at baggage claim." The sexy voice was gone. He was in work mode again. "Thanks, Eddie. I owe you one."

* * *

The double doors to the main terminal at the Toledo Express Airport slid open, and the cool air gave me a jolt, some kind of crazy-ass high that only people melting to their deaths must feel. I didn't want to move a muscle. I'd had to park in the long-term lot and walk what felt like three miles in my suit jacket. I had taken the damn thing off for the ride over, but my shirt still wasn't dry by the time I'd gotten to the airport. No way was I meeting Steven sopping wet from my own sweat. I might still stink in the jacket, but at least I wouldn't give the impression I'd run to the airport while Steven strolled off the plane looking (and smelling) fantastic, as usual. Not like a guy who'd been marinating in his own stink all day. Hell, I doubted the man even sweated during sex.

I headed for baggage claim and checked my phone. I was late. The crowd grabbing their luggage at the baggage carousels was pretty thin, but Steven was nowhere in sight. Ten minutes later I confirmed with the closest arrival board that his plane had landed on time. Still no Steven.

At least the airport was air conditioned. I waited by a vending machine selling frozen yogurt push-up pops in the various flavors of the rainbow. If Steven didn't hurry his ass up I was going to get naked and rub one of those yogurt pops all over my body. I really didn't want to get arrested. The way my luck was going, by the time I got to the jail someone would've probably had the brilliant idea to transfer the AC unit from the jail to the courthouse, and I'd be left sweating all night, still wearing the damn suit. My head throbbed again.

Maybe Steven had missed his flight. How very un-Steven-like of him.

An elderly woman with a walker shuffled toward me. She stopped in front of the vending machine and stared up at me. "It doesn't look like you're having a good day."

I gave her a smile. "I guess I'm not."

"Eddie." That voice. Definitely not Steven. I turned around.

Mike was standing ten feet away holding two bags, one in each hand. He was a few inches shorter than I, but no one would argue the fact that he had an even more dominating presence. Maybe it was the way he carried himself, holding nothing back, his chest out, arms at his sides but not relaxed, ready to engage in whatever activity was necessary at any moment. He was in a T-shirt, shorts, and a pair of leather sandals. I'd never seen him wear sandals before, no matter how hot it'd gotten outside. Was Mike changing, and I wasn't even noticing? That hurt too much to contemplate.

I made my way to him. "I thought you wanted me to pick Steven up." Dammit. I wasn't in the mood for this.

Mike didn't say anything right away. He just stood there with a weird-ass smirk on his face until he finally said, "Here." He handed me one of the bags. It looked a lot like my bag. "That's yours," he said and held up the other. "This one's mine. Our flight leaves in an hour, so we better get checked in."

"What are you talking about?"

He smiled that sexy grin that had his eyes crinkling up and meant he was seriously enjoying himself. I hadn't seen that look in a long time. "Can't a guy surprise his man after fifteen years?"

I looked at the bag in my hand, then the one in his. "We're going somewhere?"

He handed over the ticket.

"Chicago?" I asked. Although it was a stupid question since I'd read the destination off the printed ticket with my own name.

"Keep reading," he said.

Another flight. "Hawaii?"

"A private resort on Lanai. We'll get there after midnight their time. We're staying on the beach. Ocean breezes. Fifteen degrees cooler than here. Should feel damn good."

I wanted to comment on how much a trip like that must have cost, but he was weird about money. His grandpa had left him a sum that would keep him more than comfortable, but he liked earning his own way. Besides, his family had stopped speaking to him when he'd come out in his early twenties. He got a kick out of keeping the money and not touching a dime of it. A private resort? On the beach? Sounds like he finally found a reason to dip into the funds. Which blew me away. I hadn't thought there was a reason in the world why he'd spend that money. I said, "I have court on Wednesday."

"We get back late Tuesday." He stepped closer and spoke in that voice he used when discussing something serious he thought I might not like. "You need a break. *We* need a break."

Had he said those words without giving me the ticket first, I would've thought he was calling us quits. Even on the day before our anniversary. "What are we going to do when we get there?" I asked.

The smile was back. "Now that's a surprise." He'd probably found the one gay bar on the island. Which would be okay. He'd planned something just for the two of us. Something different than the usual way we spent our anniversary. I could live with one night out surrounded by a slew of strangers.

I couldn't think of anything to say, except… "Tony was talking about the party tomorrow night."

"Yeah. I told everyone to keep up appearances." He laughed. He was really enjoying this. "Come on. I brought you something to change into." The smile on his face grew with a shake of his head. "That suit has got to go."

* * *

"Aloha! Welcome to the Lanai Paradise Resort." The woman working the resort's front desk smiled at Mike while I stood a step behind him holding our bags. It was late, and the lobby was empty, except for the two of us and the clerk with the huge smile checking us in.

Mike had a way with women. They always thought he was coming on to them, and he didn't bother explaining otherwise. Maybe it was that bad-ass-tough-guy look he had going on combined with the nicest-guy-you'd-ever-meet personality. He'd give the shirt off his back (and a hell of a lot more) to anyone who needed it. Maybe that's what most women were looking for. Women usually knew what it was they wanted. Me? I hadn't a clue until I was so far gone in lust I didn't want to walk away, so I actually took the time to get to know him.

She looked up our reservation and said, "One of our honeymoon cottages. Excellent choice."

Okay, she'd seen that I was with him, knew we were sharing a room, so maybe she got that he wasn't flirting. I stared at the back of his head as he signed for the room. Not a room, though. A cottage. A honeymoon cottage on the beach. Holy shit, he'd gone all out.

Once we were checked in, a young man led us outside. Mike insisted we carry our bags. We just had the one each, and he never did like someone else doing something for him he could do for himself, even when it was an included paid service. We followed the man down a stone pathway behind the back of the resort's main building. Seven-foot-tall torches lit the way, offering a view of the surrounding foliage and small lighted ponds of colorful tropical fish. The trees and shrubs were more exotic than anything I was familiar with. It all gave the place a secluded feel. A second path veered off to the right, and in another minute we were standing before the honeymoon cottage, a small one-story building with dim lights already on inside, creating a soft glow in the darkness of the night.

Mike tipped the young man and went inside. I stepped one foot in and stopped in my tracks, dropping my bag to the floor beside me. I was speechless. Across the room was a wall made of glass, a sliding door with floor-to-ceiling windows on each side and curtains pulled back to reveal the panoramic view. The door leading to the deck was open and beyond the deck and white sand of the beach I could see it. The ocean. Even in the dark of night it was a vibrant blue, clear and sparkling under the moon's rays. The waves rolling onto the beach were hypnotic to watch. I walked straight for the doors and stared out. The moon was high, and it lit the beach and the water far beyond in the distance. The sound of the surf rushing in and out mesmerized me.

But the best part, the part I wanted to stand there until I could soak it into every molecule of my body, and could also figure out how to bottle it up and take it home with me, was the cool breeze blowing in off the ocean.

God, it felt great. Nothing like the stale, humid air in Ohio.

I could have stood there all night, watching the water foam as the waves crashed onto the shore, the wind on my face, the curtains on each side of the windows billowing out beside me.

Mike cleared his throat.

I forced myself to turn and look over the rest of the place. The cottage was one large room in a tropical decor of blues, greens, and yellows with hardwood floors and bamboo-style rugs. There were windows on every wall, including a picture window above the bed's headboard. That one king-size bed was the focal point of the room. No desk. No TV. Nothing to distract. A ceiling fan spun silently overhead. I could see a full bathroom through the open door behind Mike. The tub looked large enough for two. "This is…"

"What?" he asked as he tossed his bag on the chair beside the bed.

"Romantic."

He smiled and looked around. "Yeah, I didn't do too bad, did I?"

"I didn't know you knew how to do that."

"What?"

"Romance."

"Fucker." He smirked, and a second later he came at me. In a rush he took me in his arms and planted one hell of a kiss on my lips.

That was more like Mike.

He moved me backward out the open doors. "You need a shower."

I pointed to the door on the other side of the bed. "That's the bathroom."

"The ocean is this way." He kept moving me until we made our way across the deck. "Ever swim naked in the Pacific?" he asked.

"Never swam in any ocean, clothes or no clothes."

"It's about time we changed that."

"It's the middle of the night."

"It is," he said. "Which means it's officially our anniversary."

We'd slept on the plane or I might have argued with him that we were too tired to swim in the ocean at this hour, no matter how bright the moonlight. Hell, even without the sleep I wouldn't have said anything. He was being romantic. A moonlit anniversary swim with a naked, romantic Mike. I wasn't missing that.

"Yeah," I said. "Sleep's overrated." I didn't want to waste one minute alone with him.

He raised my T-shirt over my head and dropped it to the wood deck. With his tongue he traced the beaded tattoo that wound around my neck and down my chest. He only ever made it a few inches along that path. He moved lower to my pecs. I always got off on his lips and tongue teasing my nipples. He knew it and used that to his advantage. But it had been such a damn long time since he'd done so.

He straightened, took a step back, and stripped off his shirt. "Get undressed."

He didn't have to tell me twice, and it wasn't just because I'd been dying to sit around naked for the past twelve hours. He lowered his shorts to the deck, and I stopped with mine halfway down my thighs. Mike was hard. Seriously hard, with a drop of precum lingering at the tip of his cock. One kiss and a short suck of my nipple and he was ready to pop. Maybe he needed this trip even more than I did.

Maybe he needed me—just me—more than our usual anniversary party, more than I'd given him credit for. The relief washed over me, and the muscles in my neck and shoulders loosened as if he'd just given me an hour-long massage. Guess it hadn't been only work making me so tense.

I expected him to bend me over a piece of the matching wicker deck furniture, the table or maybe one of the oversize lounge chairs, but he didn't. He smiled again. I hadn't seen him smile this much in months. He looked like a dope with the silly grin and his dick rock hard. I didn't care. It was a stunning combination.

"Race you," he said, then jumped off the deck and ran onto the beach stark naked, heading for the water's edge.

"Asshole," I called out as I kicked off my shorts and shoes. I chased after him, laughing all the way to the water. He'd already made it in waist-high by the time I got there. He splashed me as I ran in. I lunged at him, and he let out a huge-ass giggle as I wrapped my arms around his chest from behind. A fucking giggle.

Wait. That hadn't come from him. It was from me. His laugh still sounded like a guy his size normally would. It sounded great. I sounded like a kid running to get to the dodgeball first at recess. Maybe it was the sound of pure joy.

I had every intention of dunking him under the water, but I gave up on that idea. I couldn't bring myself to end his laughter.

Better to cut off my own embarrassing sounds. I let go of him, dove under the surface, and basked in the cool water that surrounded my heated flesh from head to toe. The stickiness of the past twelve hours washed away, and every concern and worry went with it.

Maybe I had been under too long. His large hands grabbed my arms and yanked me up. "Come here." He brought his lips to mine. The stubble on his face was wet, and the water dripped to my chest as we pressed closer together.

He grabbed the back of my head and parted his lips. So many times we'd done this, a caress of tongues, the intensity building, our cocks growing harder as our bodies surged together, as we shifted our hips and found the rhythm that drove us both to the edge. But we'd never done anything outside. We'd fucked year after year in front of forty guys, but not once had he given me a simple kiss on the lips outside of our place or a gay bar. Never outdoors where someone might see. Never standing naked in the ocean.

He backed up a few steps toward the cottage tugging me along with him, never stopping the touches or the kisses until we reached the water's edge. He pulled me down to the sand until I was lying on top of him. I braced myself, hands in the wet sand on each side of his head, and lined up our bodies groin to groin. I stared down at him. The wet hair on his chest shone in the dim light of the moon. The muscles of his biceps flexed as he ran his palms down my arms. His eyes crinkled up again at the corners as he gave me a slow smile. God, he'd never looked better. The swell of the surf rolled in around us, the water shallow, barely an inch deep where he had decided to get horizontal. Such a smart man.

We moved together, creating friction that had my cock wet at the tip for reasons that had nothing to do with the ocean. I rocked faster, loving the groan he gave up as my shaft grazed the sensitive skin below the head of his dick. I didn't want the moment to end. But I also wanted the wave of orgasm to crash into us both, like the surf washing over our tangled limbs. I wanted to watch his face in the moonlight as he came.

He must have had another idea. "Eddie, stop. Up. Inside."

Maybe those were all the words he could form right then.

I figured he meant that he wanted us to go inside the cottage since he was pushing me away from him, and not that he wanted me to get my dick inside him. I stood and stared down at him as he lay in the sand, his gorgeous hard cock resting against his abs, waiting for my touch again, the taut muscles of his body reminding me of his power and strength and everything I loved about the male body—about his body. He still moved me beyond mere desire and lust like no one I'd ever known.

I couldn't wait any longer. Not once I realized I'd been standing there stroking my dick as I stared at him. I didn't want my own hand. I wanted him. I reached out and helped him stand. He kissed me, hard, fast, then grunted out the words, "More. Inside." He tugged me with him toward the cottage. He didn't stop for the table on the deck, for my bag, for his, or the bathroom. He went straight for the bed.

He threw back the thin blanket and the sheet beneath. Both caught in a gust of air and billowed out before wafting to the floor beside the bed. He climbed onto his knees in the middle of the mattress. I didn't wait for him to grunt out more one-word commands. I kneeled facing him. The lengths of our cocks touched first. He hissed, and that spurred me on. I grabbed his ass and dragged him closer until we were kissing, clutching at each other like we had on the beach.

Mike pulled away and flopped onto his back on the bed, his hard cock bobbing and slapping against him. I wanted to stuff it in my mouth, but there he went again with another idea.

He gripped my hips and forced me to straddle his thighs. He moved me forward and spread my ass until his cock nestled between my ass cheeks. Hands still clutching my hips, he helped me move up and down, rubbing my ass along his shaft. He said, "Did you notice anything special in this room?"

Huh? I was supposed to be looking at the room?

If he wanted to have a conversation, then the heat of his cock against my ass was way too distracting. I tried to focus. Okay. Headboard. Open window above. Yellow walls. White ceiling. Bedside table. Lamp. Wait…

"What is that?" I asked.

"Your favorite kind."

Talk about romantic.

Seriously.

I grabbed the bottle of lube from the table. It must have already been there when we'd arrived. I hadn't seen him open his bag. Which meant he'd arranged with the resort to have it waiting for us. Which meant he'd really given this a lot of thought.

"I didn't think they made this anymore," I said. We hadn't had any at our place in five years or more. I'd searched every sex store I could find, both in person and online.

"They do," he said. "It's just really hard to come by. Took me forever"—he thrust up and grunted—"to find a place that sold it." Which was so damn sweet when I thought of how often he'd made fun of me for being so attached to a specific brand of lube. He was thrusting up against my ass harder, faster. He grasped the tops of my thighs in both hands. "Hurry."

My hand shook as I squirted the lube into my palm. "I love Hawaii."

"Hey, it's not the island of magically-appearing lube. I searched all over for that shit."

"Such a good man." I lifted my ass and reached around behind me to slather his dick. His head fell to the pillow at the contact of my slick hand to his shaft. I swiped the remainder of the lube over my hole and held his cock up as I lowered my body to him. The head of his dick pressed against the tight ring of muscle. Fuck, I'd missed this. And not just my favorite lube. I'd missed the feel of him pushing at my body, dying to get inside me, not just to get off fast anyway we could muster the energy for. I'd missed being so damn turned on I might explode with just his dick in my ass, but wanting to make it last as long as he could stand it, wanting nothing more than him pounding into me, taking his pleasure from me.

He pushed up, an easy, gentle motion, and the head of his cock pressed inside. I waited a moment to catch my breath, for the burn to ease, then I shifted up and down, working myself onto him.

He threw his head back again and bit his bottom lip. "Yes. God, yes. Eddie!"

I surged forward to kiss him. His tongue met mine in a fierce exchange.

"I'm ready," I said.

It was a response to a question he no longer asked but that he had for weeks when we'd first started fucking. His way of making sure I was ready for what he wanted to do.

His eyes widened at my words, and that was it. In an instant he had me flipped over onto my back, my legs over his forearms, and was thrusting inside me like a man possessed with a desperate need to climax or die trying. I shifted my hips, wishing I could get his dick to hit my gland, but there'd be time for that. Later. We had four days in this paradise. And by paradise, I wasn't thinking about the resort or the island.

Mike's breaths came harder, and his face reddened as he groaned and slammed into me one last time. If any part of my brain was still working I might have tried to figure out when the last time was I'd had his cum in my ass. It didn't matter now.

He fell forward, his forehead landing on my shoulder. He was panting. His heavy breaths blew across my body, tickling my chest hair. I was content to stay that way for a while despite having my knees practically at my ears and my still-hard cock's interest in some friction. Mike had other ideas. He sat up fast, slipped from my body, and flipped us over again until I was lying on top of him.

"Up," he said.

I didn't know what he wanted, but I propped myself over him on my knees with my hands on either side of his broad shoulders. He scooted down the bed in one quick movement. I gasped as he gripped the base of my cock and his mouth sucked me in. I straightened my legs and rose up onto my toes to keep some of my weight off him. He focused on the head of my dick for a long time, wetting, swirling, sucking. My arms and legs were shaking by the time he slid his mouth over the length.

One long pull to the tip, and he released me. "You taste salty."

I almost told him it was okay to use his hand, but his next words stopped me short.

"It's okay, Eddie. Fuck me." He grabbed my ass and tugged me forward, all the way into his mouth again. I let myself go. Let my body move and thrust into the wet heat of his talented mouth. His big hands massaged my ass. One slid to caress my balls, then back again, between my cheeks, pressing at and around my hole, over and over.

When his thick finger drove inside me and hit my gland, I was a goner. "Mike!" I gave one more thrust and came, my hips making little jerking movements throughout the spasms that took hold of my body.

"Oh God." I fell to the side, trying not to land on him as my arms gave out.

He kissed my hip, his hands still massaging over the muscles of my ass. I glided my own hand over the surface of his smooth bald head and down the back of his neck, reveling in how masculine he felt when I touched him that way, how hot he looked with his cheek resting on my leg next to my spent cock. He nuzzled my balls and made his way up the bed, never letting go of me, wandering his hands over my heated skin and tracing the tats along my arm and shoulder with his tongue until we were lying face-to-face.

His eyes were half closed, but he had a satisfied grin. I probably had the same. A matching set.

It was the first time we'd done it in a bed on our anniversary. The normalcy of that may seem boring to most. Not to me. I'd been waiting years for this.

He laughed as he shifted his ass on the sheet. "God, I have sand everywhere."

I'd forgotten he'd been lying on the beach while I'd been on top of him, and I could only imagine where the sand had gotten. I laughed with him. "Uncomfortable?" I asked.

He ran a hand down my cheek. The stubble made a scratching sound against his palm. His thumb lingered over my lower lip. "Not at all," he said.

"That's a damn good lie. Come on. Let's get cleaned up." I got off the bed and dragged him up with me. He gave me a chaste kiss, then withdrew. He didn't speak. He held my face in his hands and watched me. Was I supposed to say something? His stare grew more intense, the squeeze of his palms tighter. Not painful. Intent. Serious. His eyes searched mine. "I love you."

He'd said it before. A lot over the years, in fact. Then why did those three words move me like never before? Maybe we'd gone too long without saying them. Maybe it was the beach, the skinny-dipping, the sound of the surf, the tropical breeze, my favorite kind of lube. Or maybe it was just that he always had great timing.

"Thank you," I said.

His grip on my face eased, and he smirked. "For telling you what you should already know?"

"For all this. For the trip. Everything."

"You're welcome. But tonight was only the beginning. Let's go shower, then we'll get some sleep. We have a big day tomorrow."

"Oh yeah?"

"I booked a few things so we can see the island. Then there's this bar—"

I nodded. "Sounds good." I grabbed him by the back of the neck. "I love you." My lips grazed his as I said the words, then we were kissing again, a deep, long kiss that helped me forget about whatever he had in mind for tomorrow night.

Tonight had been perfect. I could live with however he wanted to spend the rest of our anniversary.

* * *

I heard Mike's distant laughter, and that did it. I went from jogging to a flat-out run.

He must have done the same. Even the laughing wasn't slowing him down. We were nearing the stretch of beach in front of our cottage. At this rate I was never going to catch him. He was older than I, but I could already hear the old-timer comments he'd sling my way. I'd never hear the end of it if I couldn't at least close the gap.

We'd gotten up early despite our late night and had rented a four wheeler to drive to a red rock formation that changed colors under the rising sun, then we'd spent the rest of the day snorkeling and kayaking near Hulopoe Bay. The tropical fish, sea turtles, and two dolphins we caught glimpses of all afternoon fascinated Mike, and I could see he was disappointed when it was time to get out of the water. If the night before alone together had been perfection, then today had been the best damn icing on the cake I'd ever tasted. I hadn't had a headache all day. I hadn't thought about court or the case or anything else. Just the two of us and the gorgeous views.

All of it had reminded me of what I loved about Mike. How much damn fun he was to just hang with. His humor, his easy way of going with the flow, his curiosity and the thrill he got out of trying new things.

When we'd made it back to the resort we'd parked the four wheeler at the main building, slipped off our shoes and shirts, and started to walk barefoot along the beach to our cottage. Until Mike had yelled, "Race you," and taken off.

Who knew he was such a kid at heart.

I guess I did. Once upon a time. I liked him in Hawaii. Away from the bar and the stress of the construction at the restaurant.

He came to a stop and stared out over the ocean. I was out of breath when I reached his side. He turned and without a word he tackled me. We fell to the ground, both of us breathing heavily. He was on top, but I dug my heels into the sand and flipped us.

We wrestled more, rolling in and out of the surf. Neither of us had shaved since we'd left Ohio, and the rasp of his facial hair against my chest as he tried to roll me over teased my nipples. I was getting hard. I hadn't been turned on from such simple, playful aggression in a long time. I felt free, like I could breathe again, only I hadn't known I'd been holding my breath for so damn long.

We need a break.

"Hey." Mike stopped the rolling and sat up beside me. He stared out over the water again. "Check it out." The sun was setting in the distance, giving off a glow that turned the surface of the ocean blazing shades of orange and red.

I sat up and said, "I can't believe you did all this."

"You having fun?" he asked.

"I am."

He stood. "It's time to go get ready or we'll be late." He reached down and helped me up. When I was standing beside him he slipped his hand into mine and didn't let go. In fifteen years we'd never held hands. Not outside of the bedroom. I wanted this moment to go on for a while longer. I didn't want to go to some bar where we didn't know anyone, where it wouldn't be just the two of us, where he wouldn't laugh like he'd been doing all day.

But I had made a promise to myself. This one night I'd give him what he needed.

When we reached the deck I stopped. There was a small round table in the middle that hadn't been there before. It was set for two. Covered plates at each setting, candles lit in the center, and a bottle of wine off to the side.

I pointed to the table. "Are we eating first? I thought you said we'd be late."

"Yeah. For this."

"No bar?"

"No bar. I said that to throw you off the surprise. I thought this year maybe..." He looked at the table, then back to me. "Just us."

I stood staring at him for a minute, then leaped forward and grabbed him. I'd meant for it to be a hug, a show of appreciation. I hadn't meant to fling myself at him so hard we'd go flying backward. Good thing the deck was low to the ground. He landed on his back on the sand, and I came down sprawled half on top of him, half beside him.

I pulled myself up and straddled his thighs. "Are you all right?"

"Yeah. I take it you're okay with the change of plans?"

"More than okay."

He sat up and shifted us around until we were kneeling side by side watching the sunset again.

"Why did you do all this?" I asked.

"Fifteen years deserves a little something special, yeah?"

"Yeah."

He slowly looked my way, his expression serious, and then he glanced out over the water again. "We needed this. It's too easy to get swept away by life. Away from what matters most. I wanted us to be swept away together, if just for a little while." He paused, then added, "We need to do this every year. Get away. Recharge. Just us."

"Just us," I said. I looped my arm around his and placed my head on his shoulder.

He rested his temple against mine and whispered in my ear. "Happy Anniversary." I could hear it in his voice...he was smiling again.

That made two of us.

The Break-In

My foot slipped on the windowsill, and I flung through the opening feet first. I landed with my ass on the hardwood floor, my feet stuck under a dresser, and my hands twisted in the curtains.

How many times had I snuck through that window? It should've been second nature to me. I shouldn't have been slumped on the floor like the world's worst prowler.

And yet, there I was, gripping the long curtains in both fists, adrenaline rushing through me as though they were going to walk in and find me stuck in that ridiculous position. Which was stupid. I wasn't about to get caught. They had dinner out every Friday night. Not at the same restaurant, but it didn't matter where they were. It only mattered that they wouldn't be home for another couple of hours. I had time.

I untangled my hands, pushed myself off the floor, and listened for a moment. Despite my need for silence, the lack of any life inside the apartment disturbed me. I missed the sound of his laughter as he viewed the countless YouTube videos he pretended he didn't watch, the tapping on the keyboard of his laptop, his humming in the shower.

I stood still in the silent bedroom for another few breaths. The music first. It made the couple of hours I spent in the apartment seem like I was supposed to be there, like I still lived there and was doing the laundry or jogging on the treadmill. Anything but the real reason.

Down the long hall, the hardwood floor squeaked in the same places it always had. I strode past the couch we'd made love on so many times, past his recliner where he'd do his work, letting my hand linger on the worn blue fabric of the headrest. How many times had he set aside his laptop and called me to him? How many times had I curled up in his arms there?

I crossed the living room to the stereo. I didn't even check, just hit the play button and waited for the soulful jazz to break the silence.

The quiet disrupted, I crept back down the hall to the bedroom where I ignored the large bed, the visible red sheets, the comforter crumpled at the foot of the mattress. Ignoring those details would be better, wouldn't let me think things like, *nine months and he still needed me for something.*

I opened the top dresser drawer and rifled through the contents until my fingers met the soft fabric of his black briefs, the ones I had clasped between my teeth as I undressed him so many times. I laid the underwear across the top of the dresser and wrenched off my pants and T-shirt. I shivered and tried to tell myself it was the chill in the room meeting my naked body. Right.

My underwear on the floor, I slipped into his pair, trying to ignore the erection forming, the way my body warmed with the slide of the fabric. When I first started breaking in, it would take me until the end of my routine before I'd get hard. The sadness used to be too heavy; it overpowered the desire. Now, the feel of his underwear against my skin worked like a dream.

Inside the next drawer were the jeans. They were too wide, too long, but it didn't matter. It wasn't like I was going anywhere dressed like that. The clothes were for me. He'd never see me in them. The idea of him finding me dressed like that turned me on more. I pulled on his jeans and went for the closet.

I ran my hand over every shirt, every suit, every pair of slacks, loving the mental images of him in the courtroom, the command of that strong voice. The shirt I wanted to wear in my hand, I reached for the tie rack. The dark blue one. It went best with his eyes, like the last time I'd seen him in it. He'd just landed a major client and promotion, and we were celebrating at Romano's. By the end of the night, I was begging him to tie me up using only that tie. He paid the bill, and we were out the door before the waiter had a chance to bring the dessert cart. We never made it to using the tie, though. After, when he was holding me in the dark, our bodies sweat-soaked, the cum still drying on my skin, he had whispered, "Next weekend, we'll use the tie."

Too bad I'd never know what it felt like when he wound the tie around my wrists.

Too bad I had fucked up before the next weekend and had lost it all.

I glided my hand across my chest and plucked a nipple. With my other hand, I stroked myself through his jeans and bucked my hips. If I wasn't careful, I wouldn't last as long as I wanted.

Time for the rest.

His shirt on and the tie draped around my neck, I moved my private party to the bathroom. The cologne was sitting on the vanity top as if I were expected, as if he knew I visited every Friday night. When I had lived there, he kept the cologne tucked inside the medicine cabinet. I trembled as I lifted the bottle. Out of fear? Or hope?

In either case, I didn't let it linger. He didn't know about my visits. If he had, he would've called the cops. Or my parole officer. No, he would've confronted me.

I opened the bottle and splashed cologne on my neck. My skin tingled with the memory of his hands on me. I buried my nose in my palm. Never did smell the same on me. I'd give anything to smell it on him. One more time.

No. I'd give anything to have it all back—the sex, the long talks in bed, the laughter, the love. But it would never be like that.

I'd never live in that apartment again. Never make love in that bed. Never be held in those strong arms. I had to accept that. And someday, I would. I'd stop the breaking and entering every Friday night. But not yet.

It was a small change that caught my eye, but it was enough to startle me. The bottle of lube kept inside the shower was now in the soap dish, not the shower caddy. Had they purposely decided to store it somewhere new, or had they accidentally left it there? Had they been in the shower together that morning? Fucking each other?

Had it been Roger inside Doug?

Or the other way around?

I couldn't stop the memories: my forehead pressed against the glass door as he took me from behind; those large hands on my hips, on my chest, on my cock; me on my knees and his dick in my mouth—just the way he liked after a long day at work. He called my mouth the best stress relief he'd ever had. I'd never been anyone's best anything before.

Never would again. All because of one mistake. The worst of my life.

Since I was twelve, my mom had said I'd end up in prison. Who knew she'd be right? I had thought finding the love of my life had meant the end of the bad shit, the beginning of a new life.

If only I hadn't gone out that night.

If only I had done what he wanted—stayed in, decorated the tree, listened to Christmas carols, made love to "Moon Dreams" by Miles Davis.

If only I hadn't believed my best friend when he said we wouldn't get caught.

But I knew what an empty belly felt like. I knew what it was like to live on the streets, turning tricks for a meal.

I scrubbed a hand over my face before the tears could form and reached for the lube they had moved since my last visit. I placed it on the top shelf of the shower caddy. I'd move it back before I left, but something inside me couldn't leave it alone. I needed it to be where we had kept it.

Not where they did.

Back in the bedroom, I didn't want to look at the bed, didn't want to see the mussed covers, the sheets twisted in a way that only meant one thing had last happened there. I kept my eyes squeezed shut as I crawled to the center of the bed. My erection had subsided with the memories of how I'd lost it all, but the sound of the smooth jazz and the scent of him on the pillows aroused me again. I shifted my hips and reached for the top button of the too-big jeans.

I froze with the sound of the front door opening. Their laughter poured into the apartment, blending with the cool, passionate jazz. It sounded like laughter at a wake. It mocked me. The sound track of my life.

Hyperventilation set in. Why were they home early?

Their laughter grew louder. I needed to get up and out the window. Why couldn't I move?

"You leave the music on?" That was Doug. His soothing voice always got to me. I missed hearing it mix with his laugh, hearing him whisper all the sexy, delicious things he wanted to do to me.

"Don't know. Maybe," Roger said. His voice grew louder. "Must have."

Why did he have to sound sexy too?

I scrambled for the edge of the bed and scooped up the clothes I'd worn to break in. Their footsteps approached the bedroom door. No time to change.

The doorknob turned.

No time for anything.

I dropped to the floor and crawled under the bed, the big-ass jeans getting all tangled up, making it hard to move. The blue tie must have slipped off me. It lay on the floor beside the bed. I grabbed it, and the door swung in. I jerked my hand back and clutched the tie to my chest.

Doug stepped in first. The dark cowboy boots were the same ones he wore every day, even under the suits. His feet turned as Roger came in close. The sound of their kisses filled the room.

Oh God. They were going to make love with me underneath the goddamn bed.

A tie fell to the floor three feet from my face. Doug's tie. His dress shirt followed, a crumbled pool of fabric around their ankles.

Yep. I was going to be stuck under the bed listening to them go at each other. The thought should've unnerved me. And it did, in a way, but it also turned me on. I would get to hear him moan and beg. Hear him cry out as he came.

Another shirt fell to the floor, and both men toed off their boots and socks. They kissed again, the sloppy sounds mixing with Doug's little hums. God, how I missed that.

"Love you." That was Roger. Those whispered words brought tears to my eyes. I wiped them away. I would not cry. I would enjoy the moment for what it was—me listening to two hot guys having sex. It couldn't be anything more.

"Tell me." Roger again.

"No," Doug said. He took a step back from Roger, his bare feet coming even closer to the edge of the bed—to me. "You promised me we wouldn't talk about it again."

Roger stepped forward. Their limbs mingled together. "I think we need to talk about it," Roger said. "Talk about him."

Him? Someone new?

They kissed again, the sound more enticing than before. My heart thundered in my chest. I wanted to crawl out from under the bed, fly out the window, and race along the city streets until I collapsed from exhaustion.

"Tell me," Roger said.

Doug sighed. "I miss him."

I squeezed my eyes shut and tried to keep my breathing even, to keep still. Was Doug talking about me?

"Of course you do," Roger said.

"But we can't."

"Why not? He's sorry."

"How do you know that?"

"Don't tell me you don't know what he's been doing."

Fuck.

Roger stepped around Doug until his feet and lower legs framed Doug's from behind. Together they moved as one toward the dresser. With the change in their location, I could see all of them. Both were shirtless. Roger in jeans, the fabric clinging to the muscles of his thick thighs. Doug in dress slacks, his taut, slimmer frame nestled back against Roger. I clutched my clothes tighter to my chest.

Roger reached around Doug and pulled open the top drawer. "He likes to put on your underwear. The black ones. He always puts them back before he goes, but they still smell like him hours later. They smell like his need, your soap, and my cologne. They smell like the three of us."

Oh God. I buried my face in my clothes. They knew what I did every time I snuck in. Did they know the rest? I forced myself to look again.

Doug dropped his head back to Roger's shoulder, wound his arms around Roger, and squeezed the firm ass cheeks.

"I bet he likes to feel your underwear against his skin." Roger whispered the words into Doug's ear. "Imagine it's you touching him. I bet he gets hard just thinking about it." Roger rotated his groin over Doug's ass. "Hard as I am now."

Were they angry? No. They were turned on. As turned on as I was, so fucking hard I wanted to shove my hand inside the pair of underwear Roger was talking about.

Roger opened another drawer. "He wears my jeans."

Doug wasn't saying anything. He was moving, rubbing back against Roger, running his hands over Roger's ass.

Then Roger moved the two of them toward the closet, and still holding Doug from behind, he slid open the door and turned on the light. Just as I had done a few minutes earlier—only without the holding Doug part.

"I bet," Roger said, "he touches himself as he picks out one of your ties."

Doug removed a hand from Roger's ass and ran the tips of his fingers over the line of dress shirts. Those graceful fingers moved in such a slow, gentle touch, and I almost moaned out loud. I bit my lip and shifted my hips, my cock getting a little friction with the move. I wanted more. I wanted them.

Roger worked a hand down the front of Doug's pants and began a slow, sensual stroke. I ached to feel Roger's hands on me, Doug's lips against mine, my body pressed between them. One last time.

"He picks out a shirt." Roger continued the movement of his hand on Doug's cock. "One of my dress shirts. And your blue tie."

Doug gasped.

"The one we were going to use on him the night we celebrated your promotion. The night he'd begged us to tie him up. The night we last made love."

Doug wiped his eyes. Was he crying? His voice was shaky when he finally spoke. "We never did get to the tie."

"No. But we said we would." Roger gripped Doug's hand in his and led the way across the room. "After he dresses in our clothes, he goes to the bathroom."

I shifted until I could see them through the open doorway. They stood in front of the mirror. Roger reached around Doug again and lifted the bottle of cologne. He opened it and poured some into the palm of his hand. He worked his hands together in front of Doug, and then spread the cologne over Doug's cheeks and down his neck. Doug's hips were moving again.

Roger kissed the skin of Doug's neck from earlobe to shoulder. I could almost smell Doug's skin, the mix of arousal and Roger's cologne. I had never smelled that cologne on Doug. Did they smell the same wearing it?

Roger ran his hands down the front of Doug's naked chest, over one nipple then the other, progressed lower and lower, and finally, dipped a hand into the front of Doug's pants. I panted at the thought of smelling Roger's cologne on Doug's cock and balls.

I watched the fabric of Doug's pants move with the hand working him. I gulped down a swallow and tried to remember how to breathe.

Roger's gruff voice startled me. "Now we all smell the same."

Doug moaned and shifted his hips faster.

"Come to bed, lover." Roger eased his hand out of Doug's pants and turned for the door. He stopped and laughed as he grabbed the bottle of lube from the shower. "He didn't like us leaving the lube somewhere new."

"Why?" Doug asked.

"I think he misses the way we did things. The way we were together—the three of us. He's miserable alone."

"He left us—"

"You know why." Roger held Doug against his chest and whispered to the hair above Doug's ear. "He thought we'd be ashamed of him. He thought coming home to us from prison would make us love him differently. He thought he was an extra we were playing with, and that we'd be fine without him. That we'd go right back to where we were before we found him outside the club. He doesn't know he was as much a part of this relationship as either of us. He doesn't know how easily it was for that hungry, lonely man to steal our hearts."

I couldn't stop the tears that streamed down my face. Roger's words penetrated every inch of thick skin I had been trying to build since I'd left them for prison.

It was odd—hiding under the bed we had once shared, wearing their clothes, crying like I never had in my life, and yet my cock hard, my body so hungry for them, I didn't know if I'd be able to walk away if they discovered me and demand I leave. But it didn't sound like they would. They still wanted me.

Maybe I had already jerked off and had fallen asleep on the red sheets, and their words were my wishes come to life in my dreams.

They moved as one to the middle of the bedroom, facing each other.

Doug glanced toward the closet. "Where's the tie? It wasn't in there."

"We came home early enough."

Doug's mouth fell open. "He's here?"

Roger nodded.

I hugged my clothes tighter to me and held my breath.

"Where?"

Roger looked over his shoulder. "Under the bed."

Doug turned, and both men stared at me.

I knew I wasn't dreaming because I used all my mental powers to force the floor to split open and swallow me whole. It didn't.

"Billy?"

I should've been man enough to crawl out and face them, but my name on Doug's lips had me frozen under the bed, holding my own clothes, wearing theirs, tears on my face, and my dick rock hard.

Doug walked to the bed, crouched beside it, and lifted the sheet hanging over the edge. "Billy, come out here." Those blue, blue eyes were watching me.

Roger hadn't moved from where he stood, but his voice was louder than any of his words since he'd stepped into the apartment. "Billy."

That was all it took. I never could resist his requests, not in the bedroom. He liked to lead the way. And I always liked to let him. So did Doug. Roger said it was because Doug needed to let go of the control he held on to all day in the courtroom. And he said I needed to give all of myself to someone.

He was right about that.

I worked my way out from under the bed, still not letting go of my clothes. I might need them before long.

Doug wrapped a hand around my upper arm and helped me stand, the baggy jeans making the move an issue, my nerves adding to it.

The soft touch of Doug's hand on my arm and the comforting blue eyes watching me took me back in time to the first night I'd met them, when they'd driven me to a diner and fed me a roast beef sandwich with extra fries, had brought me home and ran me a hot bath, and then had taken me to their bed where nothing close to sex happened and where I slept pressed between them. The next day, they'd had a new bed delivered for the guest room. It took three months before either of them kissed me. Another two before they brought me to their bed again. I learned later, they had wanted to wait even longer. They didn't want me to feel like I owed them something.

But it had never felt like that. All I ever felt was their love.

I stared at Doug's hand on my arm. I longed to feel the heat of his palm on my skin. Why couldn't I have jerked off naked in their bed? Only that would have also put me naked standing before them. I already felt exposed. Vulnerable. Like the twenty-something kid from the street they'd brought home with them five years before.

Doug yanked me forward and crushed me against his chest. "Stupid, stupid man."

Roger stood behind me and wound his large arms around us, pinning me between them.

All my resolve went out the window—where I should have been following it. I dropped the clothes and wrapped an arm around Doug's waist, the other back around Roger's.

Doug let out a soft moan. He buried his nose in my hair. "You've been out for two months. Where have you been staying?"

I wanted to answer, but the words caught in my throat.

Roger gripped my hip. "Billy," he said. "Where?"

I dropped my head back to his chest. "The Third Street Mission."

Doug ran a hand over my cheek. I closed my eyes and leaned into his touch.

"Why didn't you come home?" he asked.

I couldn't stop myself. I turned my head and kissed his palm.

He wiped the last of my tears from my eyes. "Did you think we wouldn't want you anymore?"

I nodded.

Roger bent and kissed the back of my neck. He worked his way to my earlobe. "Did you think we wouldn't still love you?"

A part of me knew they would, but I had wanted better for them—better than me.

Roger kissed my temple. "Talk to us."

"I was in prison." My voice trembled with each word.

Roger laughed. That deep rumble vibrated against my back. Without a thought, I shifted between them, my ass to Roger's cock, my dick to Doug's, back and forth, the rhythm coming back to me as effortlessly as any step I'd taken to get to the apartment.

Doug started to move with me, but Roger stilled our actions.

So stupid. I shouldn't have been so bold. I had left them. I had packed a bag and walked out the door while they were at work, and I had stayed at the mission until it was time to report to court. They had shown up that day. Doug wouldn't take no for an answer when he took the place of the public defender. I owed Doug years of my life. My sentence wouldn't have been as light if he hadn't shown up to help me.

And this was how I repaid them?

Breaking into their place, rifling through their belongings, trying to rub off on them as if nothing had changed between us?

Roger's deep voice sounded small when he spoke. "You

wouldn't talk to us at your court appearance. You refused to see us at the prison. You get out and don't bother to tell us where you are. Don't you think all that hurt?"

"Roger. Don't." Doug massaged my arms. "He's here."

Roger shoved a hand inside the loose pants that hung from my body. He gripped my cock. "He's here to jerk off. Not to see us."

"I-I want—" I squeezed my eyes shut.

Roger slid his hand down the length of my cock. He caressed my balls. "Say it, Billy."

I groaned and moved my hips again. "I wanted to see you. But-but you deserve better."

"Better than you?" With the surprise in Doug's voice, I opened my eyes and watched him. He searched my face. "God, Billy. You were trying to help him."

"But I stole."

Roger cupped my balls, his touch gentle, loving. "Why didn't you ask us for help? We would've given him the money."

I twisted in their arms until I could look up at Roger. "I couldn't take anything else from you."

"Take?" Roger said. "You have no clue, do you? We were missing something until we met you. We needed you as much as you needed us."

Doug forced me to look his way. "And without you, we're not whole. We're broken."

"You've punished yourself enough," Roger said. "It's time to come home."

Doug leaned forward and kissed me. His warm tongue caressed mine. All worries, all thoughts were gone. I wrapped my arms around his neck and stood on the tips of my toes. Roger's warmth left my back. I wanted to cry out, wanted to plead for his touch again, but I couldn't tear myself from Doug's kiss. I wanted him to consume me, to take my breath into him until we weren't sure where he ended and I began.

Roger pressed against my back again. One of his hands gripped my hip. The fingers of the other caressed my lower lip. I opened my mouth wider and let his thumb slide between my lips, alongside Doug's tongue until I could taste them both.

Roger slipped his thumb from my mouth and gripped one of my arms from around Doug's neck. He wound something around my wrist.

The blue tie.

I gasped.

Doug smiled at me, his lips still moist from the kiss. "You aren't getting away from us this time."

Roger laughed and tugged me backward. I trembled.

"Get naked, Doug," Roger said.

Doug stripped. I couldn't take my eyes off the hard lines of his body, the swollen erection between his legs.

Roger stepped in front of me. He forced my head up until I met his stare. "You are staying. Unless you tell me you want to go." He waited a moment, then added, "I thought not." He leaned forward and stopped, his lips an inch from mine. "I'm going to kiss the hell out of you, and I might not be able to stop once I start." He pulled back.

I whimpered. I wanted his lips on mine.

"First things first," he said. "On the bed, Doug."

Doug nodded and lay on his back in the center of the large bed.

"Arms over your head."

Doug stretched his arms up as if reaching for the headboard. His body was spread out over the red sheets like a decadent dessert offering. I wanted to crawl on top of him and take a taste. More than a taste. I wanted to devour all of him.

Roger moved behind me. He popped the top button of the jeans I wore and slid down the zipper. Doug licked his lips as he watched from the bed, his body held immobile by only Roger's will.

"Go ahead," Roger said as he continued to undress me. "Say it."

Say what? He worked the pants off me, then unbuttoned the shirt. My head spun with the brush of his large hands against my skin.

Doug spoke. "I want you so much, Billy. Missed seeing your body, touching you. Missed you between us, your smile, your laugh, your love. Missed you every moment you were gone."

Doug shifted his hips but kept his arms stretched overhead. "Been dreaming about you inside me."

Shallow breaths were all I could manage.

Roger slid the shirt off my shoulders, working it over the tie still wrapped around my wrist. He brushed the flesh of my ass and thighs as he peeled the black underwear off my body.

"God, babe," Doug said. "You're gorgeous. Come here."

He knew I wouldn't move. Not until Roger told me to. It was a game we had played many times.

He didn't give up. "Babe, crawl on top of me. Need to feel your body on mine, your tongue in my mouth, your cock inside me."

I nodded. It was all I could give him. For now.

Roger chuckled. I heard him unzip his pants. Then his muscular, naked body came in close, his arms around my chest, the solid, heated flesh of his cock at my lower back. I groaned and leaned my head back to him.

He kissed my neck. "Do I need to get a rubber?"

Huh? I lifted my head and stared at Doug on the bed. He was either enjoying the sight of my cock, or he couldn't face me.

It hit me then. "No!"

Doug closed his eyes and swallowed.

I couldn't stand still any longer. I turned in Roger's arms. "I didn't have sex with anyone else. I swear, I didn't. Just…just a couple of blowjobs. At…at…"

He cupped my cheek and ran his thumb over my lower lip. "In the prison?"

I nodded.

"I believe you." Louder, he said, "Doug?"

"Me too."

Roger gave one more swipe to my lip. He released my face and forced me to turn. "Go to him. Lie flat over his body."

I crawled onto the bed and worked my way up Doug. We both moaned as I lowered myself over him. I rested a hand on the bed on either side of his shoulders and rocked, letting our cocks and bodies get reacquainted, remembering the sweet, easy way we had been together.

Doug moaned again. The sound was beautiful and enticing. I

wanted more. I rocked faster, playing him like an old guitar, wanting to hear the same melody I'd been missing for months.

Roger grabbed my hips and tugged me backward. "Not yet. Kneel between his legs." Doug spread his thighs, and I did as Roger directed. Roger knelt behind me, the touch of his chest to my back brought out my own song, little whimpers I couldn't dream of silencing.

Roger slid his hands up the inside of Doug's thighs. "Raise your legs."

Doug lifted his legs, and with a touch of Roger's hand to my lower back, I inched closer until my cock nestled against Doug's ass. Soon I'd be inside him. And Roger would be in me. I'd be home. Finally.

Forever?

I gripped the outside of Doug's thighs, needing to touch more of him.

"Left hand, Doug."

Doug raised his hand. Roger lifted the end of the blue tie still dangling from my right wrist and wrapped it around the headboard, then both our wrists, binding us together. We entwined our fingers. Roger secured the end of the blue fabric, but it was too loose. I'd slip free before long.

"Tighter."

Roger licked my ear from top to bottom and whispered, "Tied down or not, you are not going anywhere."

"No." I let my head fall to his shoulder. "I want to stay."

"Billy." Doug squirmed and pressed his ass against my cock. I couldn't enter him. Not yet.

Roger leaned to the nightstand for the lube. He slid a hand between Doug and me and slicked my cock, then Doug's body. Doug gripped the headboard with his free hand.

"It's okay," Roger said. "Touch him. Hold on to him."

Doug let go of the headboard and reached for me under his raised leg. He gripped my thigh.

With Roger's hand guiding my cock, I pressed my pelvis forward and sank into Doug through several small thrusts. The tight slide of flesh on flesh was almost too much. I'd never be able to hold off for long. Doug groaned and squeezed my hand and thigh, his gaze locked on mine.

It had been too long since I'd been inside either of them, since I'd felt anything on my dick but my own hand. I leaned over him more and rested my free hand on the bed beside his head. I needed the leverage to fuck him the way I wanted to—the way I needed to.

No. That wasn't true. Roger would be shoving into me soon, and he'd fuck us through the mattress.

Roger spread my ass cheeks. I stilled, and he ran the slick head of his cock from the top of my ass, down the crease ever so slowly. The moment he touched my hole, he thrust forward, driving me farther into Doug.

I cried out, "Yes," and grunted over and over as he made love to us. Maybe I had missed my own sounds more than theirs. Being pinned between them was a need I'd tried to pretend I no longer craved, that I could live without.

I didn't want to come. And at the same time I'd never wanted anything more than that release.

Roger slid a hand under the silk tie around my wrist until he was bound to us—with us. He cupped my cheek with his other hand and forced my head to the side. "Kiss me." Then his lips were on mine. The sweetest brush of moist lips and tongue. Soft. Inviting. Deep. Maybe he really had meant he'd never stop kissing me. I wasn't sorry.

Abruptly, he pulled back and said, "You are not going anywhere. Tonight. Or any other night. You're ours, and we're not letting you go."

He thrust again and again, reaching around me to take Doug in his hand. We rocked and grunted, stroked and sped, loved and breathed as we flew toward release. I came first, then Roger and Doug almost together. We collapsed in a pile, Roger half on me, half wrapped around me, Doug on my other side.

Roger sighed. "Damn. You always were a sweet fuck."

I laughed and smacked his arm. "I'm feeling the love."

He sat up so fast the bed creaked. He leaned over me. "You should. And next time, don't run from it."

I nodded, and Roger sank back to the bed.

Doug reached for the blankets and lifted them over us. "Sleep."

I could do that. I hadn't been so relaxed since the night before I'd been arrested.

"Billy," Roger said.

"Huh?"

"I think we had a break-in. They left the window open."

I laughed again. Leaving the window open had been my reminder I had to leave. When I jerked off on their sheets, it was easy to focus on my cock and forget my heart. Forget I didn't belong there.

I threw the covers back, lunged for the window across the room, and tripped. I landed on the floor with my feet stuck in the twisted blanket and my hands gripping the long curtains on either side of the window.

Doug laughed, cackled, whatever you called it when someone couldn't sit up and was clutching their gut while the laughs poured out.

Roger shifted to the foot of the bed and peered down at me. "Are you okay?"

"Yeah. I am now." I kicked off the blanket, stood, and slammed the window shut. The faint sounds of honking horns, the hum of the traffic, the occasional shout disappeared. All I heard was the slowing laughter behind me and the low, deep voice that said, "You're home, Billy."

I went to the bed and settled in between them.

Roger wrapped his arms around Doug and me, pulling us all close. "You didn't have to break in. This was always your home."

I nodded.

I was home.

A Lesson in Truth

"I can't do this anymore."

"Do what?" I asked. My voice squeaked in a way that bothered me almost as much as his words.

"You know what," Michael said, his gaze focused on the stapled pages of my latest chapters lying before him, a red pen in his hand as if he was going to grade my work with me sitting right there.

I stared at him, hoping to hell he'd say more without me needing to add anything else to the conversation. The squeak was bound to emerge again. No need to remind him I was fifteen years his junior. Squeaking might give him a clue.

He ditched the pen with a flick and ran his hand through his hair. The dark strands popped up and gave his hair a spiky guise that made him look too young to be a tenured professor, too vulnerable to be telling me we were over. We hadn't even started. One kiss. One long, beautiful kiss that ruined me for all other men and he was calling it quits?

"I've asked Professor Shields to take you on," he said. "He's familiar with your thesis and knows the field of research well enough."

My stomach did a flip-flop thing I could only recall it doing one other time in my life—waiting in my dad's car as he took my dog into the vet's office for the last time. Was I going to vomit like I did then? Was I going to lose it sitting across from Michael, his metal desk between us, a wall of ungraded midterms blocking the way? I'd been in his office every week for the past two years. How did I not know where the trash can was?

"David, you're not saying anything."

Yeah, I wasn't. I was busy holding down the Cap'n Crunch I'd inhaled for dinner. That's what I got for eating a kids' cereal. Why'd I buy that shit anyway? Because I had no self control. I never could turn down what I desired—no matter how bad it was for me.

"David." That was his professor voice. The one he used when someone else was within hearing distance. Not the one he'd used for the past year. Not the one he used when we were alone. He was leaning his elbows on the desk, his eyes wide, the spiky hair still an issue, but the vulnerability the mussed hair had caused was gone. Or maybe it had been my imagination.

"What?" I said. "You want me to work with someone else? Fine."

"Don't say it like that. You know I don't have any other choice."

"Right."

"We kissed last night. Do you want to pretend that didn't happen?"

Was he crazy? I'd waited two years to feel his lips on mine. Nothing he said would erase it from my memory. Even if he wanted to forget. Even if he wanted to believe we hadn't been more than professor and student, more than friends, for a long time.

I forced myself out of the chair. I was a half-step from the door. Then why couldn't I make a move toward it?

Because this was it. I had lost my chance with him. Lost the possibility of having both a friend and a lover, having a partner who understood me like no one I'd ever dated, who was smart and funny and the sexiest man I'd ever known.

I reached for the printed chapters I had handed him five minutes earlier. No way was I leaving them behind. He was done being my advisor. He was done being my best friend. Done being my anything. The papers rattled with the shake of my hand.

Michael stood and stepped around the desk. "God, babe. Come here." He didn't wait for me to move. He came to me and pulled me against him, holding me in his arms.

I dropped the pages as he traced an invisible path up and down my back.

"I didn't think it would upset you this much." Not his professor voice. Could he just stop fucking talking?

Apparently not.

"I don't want to hurt you."

I lowered my head to his shoulder. Two years I had waited to be in his arms and this was all I was ever going to get. I turned toward his neck and breathed deep. He smelled of the cologne he always wore, but it was stronger from this distance. Almost as strong as when I wore the same stuff on the weekends—an action that gave me a bit of a stalker vibe, but I didn't care. I wanted to smell him on my sheets. Apparently it had been a wise choice. That was the only way I was ever going to have his scent there.

I searched out his skin with my tongue. The salty, rich taste burst into my mouth. I craved more. I opened wider and sucked in the warmth of him.

"God, David." He gripped the back of my head. Was he going to make me stop? He held me against him and tilted his head back.

I wound my arms around his waist and took one small step until our bodies smashed together, leaving not an inch of air between us.

Michael moaned.

Good thing his room was at the end of a long hall. Good thing it was too late for office hours.

The soft sound surged adrenaline and lust throughout my body. My dick filled, and I worked my way to his lips.

The kiss wasn't soft and slow like the one the night before. It was a kiss between two men who'd spent a damn long time dreaming of this moment, both turned on and ready to feel something more, ready to consummate a year-long love affair we had tried to pretend didn't exist.

Only I hadn't pretended as much as he. I had let myself imagine it all—the touching, the lovemaking, the nights spent in his bed.

Oddly, the one daydream I hadn't pictured was us fucking in his office.

The mental images spurred me on. I wanted him to lay me over his desk, his laptop and the stack of midterms pushed aside, and do every beautiful, naughty thing I'd been dreaming of until I screamed his name.

Michael touched the side of my face and retreated from the kiss.

That was it, then. The last taste I'd ever have.

He still held my face in his hand, though. Until he moved his hand lower. And lower. He reached the bottom of my shirt and gripped the fabric in both fists. He tugged the shirt over my head. "I want to feel you." He threw off his own shirt. "Been dying to feel your body against mine."

His hands on my bare chest took away any resistance I could've voiced. I didn't care what it all meant for him. I wanted it.

I wanted him.

He came to me as if not even a call from the university president could've stopped him. Our mouths joined again, his arms tight around me, his hands touching me in all the places I'd longed for him to be.

My heart raced at the press of his erection against my groin. I glided my hands down his arms, loving the heated flesh, the fine muscles that reminded me he didn't always sit at his desk grading papers.

"I want you." Definitely not his professor voice.

A tremble worked through me and my hands shook. "I want you too."

He ran a hand through my hair. "It's okay, David. We don't have to."

Yeah, he was crazy.

I took a step back and reached for the laptop on his desk. I set it and his favorite coffee mug on top of a short bookcase.

He shoved everything else, stack of midterms included, aside. Pens, sticky notes, paper clips, and a stapler fell to the floor. The clattering of the office supplies barely made a sound over my own deep breaths. The top of his desk sat bare before us.

I undid the zipper on my jeans.

Michael stared at me. Then his gaze dropped to where I worked my pants open, and his breath hitched. Maybe this was what he'd been dreaming of—a quick fuck in his office.

He stilled my hands. "Wait." He stepped closer. "Let me." He parted the opening of my jeans, and without removing more of my clothes, he dipped his hand inside my briefs.

I arched into the touch. The warmth of his palm around my cock could no way be compared to the two years of jerking off I'd done waiting for this moment.

He met my lips with his again. I gripped his biceps, and my hips matched the rhythm of our tongues. The sweet surrender of kissing him made me dizzy.

He stilled my body with a hand to my hip. "Wait."

He had to quit telling me to stop. A point would come when stopping would be impossible. Hell, who was I kidding? We'd already reached that stage.

He undid his dress pants and shoved them and his underwear off, kicking them away with his shoes and socks.

I froze at the sight of his hard cock. The flushed, stretched skin gave beauty new meaning. The solid flesh couldn't hide his desire. Neither could the husky voice.

"Take off your pants."

My hands shook more as I undressed. Once I stood naked, he hauled me to him again. His body tight to mine, from chest to shin, was better than any fantasy, better than any other sexual moment in my life.

He took both our cocks in his hand and stroked. "Been waiting to feel you like this." His voice had grown deeper than ever before. "Been waiting to taste you too."

Sounded good to me. I captured his mouth with another kiss and caressed his tongue with mine. Never had such a simple coming together of mouths spun my desire so out of control.

"My, God," he said. "You can kiss. But I actually meant something else." He took a step forward, moving us as one until the back of my thighs smacked against the desk. "Lie down."

I slid my ass across the desktop and tried not to shiver. It was the cool surface on my heated skin. That was all. It wasn't Michael standing naked before me.

Sure.

I lowered my body until I was lying flat before him.

He reached out and brushed the inside of my thigh with his fingers, the touch soft and tender. "Damn, you're gorgeous," he said.

The shiver was back.

He hunched over me and stopped with his mouth an inch from my dick. He met my stare and smiled before he traveled the last fragment of space separating us and lowered his mouth over the tip of my cock.

Oh God. Michael's mouth. I closed my eyes and took his head in my hands, needing to touch him. I caressed him as he worked his wet tongue down my shaft.

He began a slow pull with his lips, wetting, sucking, bringing me closer and closer to the edge. A low moan echoed in the small room. Was that me? No squeaking there.

I threw my eyes open and raised my head to watch. No way was I missing another second. His head bobbed faster. His hot lips grazed my flesh with each lift. Damn. He was good. How much practicing had he done in his life? He had probably sucked his first cock while I was learning to crawl.

It didn't matter.

There's no one else here with him now. Only me.

I quivered again as my orgasm advanced, then gave up on watching and dropped back to the desk.

Michael released me and said, "Don't come. Not yet." He rose up over me and lowered his body to mine. "Been waiting too long to be inside you." He leaned over the side of the desk, fumbled with the bottom drawer, and returned with a condom and lube. How many times had he done it in his office?

Who cared.

But I did care. Too much.

"I want to see you when you come," he said. Then his fingers were where I wanted them to be, easing the way, slicking me, then himself.

Oh, God. He was going to be inside me soon.

I lifted my legs, opening myself until he could sink into where I'd been needing him most.

That wasn't quite true, though. He'd been where I needed him for a long time. In my heart.

Michael bent over me; his strong arms framed my shoulders. His cock pressed between my ass cheeks but not inside me yet.

"David." He nuzzled my chin with his cheek. His breath traveled along my jawline as he said my name again. It mixed with a long moan. He kissed me.

I wrapped my arms around him and tugged him closer, driving my tongue deeper, trying to get him in me. I bucked my ass upward, and his hips jerked forward. Finally, he eased off my chest, took his own cock in hand, and lined up. I bit my lip as he sank deep. The sweet burn had my toes curling.

He froze. How could he hold still? Didn't he want to fuck me?

He slanted his upper body over me again. One hand gripped the edge of the desk. The other he brought to my mouth. He caressed my lip until I released it from between my teeth.

"I want to hear you," he said.

What? My moans? My pleas for more? If I let those out, I might let loose so much more.

He kissed me again and moved in a slow rock. He was everywhere. My mouth. My ass. My heart. And I wanted it all. I wanted all of him.

He gave me one last, slow kiss then he pulled back and took my legs in his hands as he set to showing me how inadequate all my other lovers had been.

How could he give this up?

How could he not want to take a chance?

Because he had his entire career to think about. *And because I'm just a college kid he has a hard-on for.* Nothing special. Nothing to take a chance on. We'd been tap dancing around this possibility for a long time, and I had let myself hope it meant to him what it did to me. I'd let myself think all the nights and weekends we'd spent together outside of the classroom—the Saturday morning pick-up basketball games, the Sunday beers with lunch, the late-night on-line chats—had meant we were dating.

I should have transferred to another advisor—hell, to another school—long before we could get to the sex on his desk part. Because having him in me, around me, all over me was going to make walking away harder than it would've been a few minutes before.

But we'd gone too far. Nothing could've stopped me.

He wrapped a hand around my shaft, and something inside me short-circuited. I came as the words I swore myself I'd never say poured out. "Love you, Michael. Loved you for so long." No wonder I ate a kids' cereal. I sounded like a babbling teenager with his first crush. I clamped my mouth shut and gripped his thighs as he thrust into me again and again.

He came with one word on his lips. "David." He collapsed onto me, and his body shuddered.

I held him. I wanted to stay that way all night, but there was the matter of the condom.

And the fact that he'd broken up with me, if I could call it that.

He lowered my legs, and I groaned as he left my body. From the physical sensation? Or from knowing he'd never be within me again, that we'd never have this moment again?

Michael draped his body over mine. His heavy breaths hit the side of my neck. "I knew," he said. "I knew it'd be good, but I had no idea..."

I shook again. Not from the cold. Couldn't even try to lie on that one. Why did he have to say anything?

He angled himself alongside me and leaned on his elbow, his legs entwined with mine, his abdomen solid against me. Why was his desk so damn small?

He ran a hand across my chest. "Are you okay?"

I slid off the desk and reached for my pants, not bothering with my underwear. "I'll go now."

"Go? Jesus, maybe I am too old for you. I thought there'd be some cuddling after. Thought you'd come spend the weekend at my place."

I froze, my pants halfway up my thighs, my briefs still lying on the floor next to my bare feet. "What are you talking about?"

He sat up. Damn, he was beautiful, his skin a temptation I ached to touch again.

"What do you think happened here?" he asked.

I spotted my thesis on the floor. It had landed on the long edge of the pages, forming a little white pop-up tent. Maybe I could crawl underneath it and hide. Anything to avoid conversation. He already told me we were done. Did he need to drag it out? But that's how he always was—concerned about my feelings, asking if I was working too hard, if I was getting enough sleep, if I'd bothered to eat a fruit or vegetable in the past week.

I met his stare. "You were saying good-bye."

He stood and slipped on his pants. Then he came to me. He grabbed the waistband of my jeans and drew them up. "I can't be with you and continue to serve as your advisor. It's unethical."

I shook my head. They were the words I'd feared since I had accepted I was in love with him. He was too good, too upstanding, too entrenched in his job to fuck a student. Even if I was done taking his classes, I was still a student in his department.

But we had fucked. No. Scratch that. We'd made love. And that's why his words were killing me even more than when I'd first stepped into his office.

He took my face in his hands. "You're so smart, sometimes I forget how young you are." He ran the pad of his thumb over my lower lip. The way he had when he'd been buried inside me. "Babe, I'm in love with you. And I'm not about to give you up. So I'm going to have to give up being your advisor. I've scheduled a meeting with the dean for Monday morning. I was hoping since you're done with your coursework and we hadn't slept together yet, this wasn't going to get me fired." He smiled. "I guess that plan's out the window."

The flip-flop thing in my stomach was back. And I hadn't found the damn trash can yet.

He loved me.

He wanted to keep seeing me.

He was going to get fired because of me.

"Oh God." I made for the chair. My feet got tangled in something—my underwear on the floor—and I pitched forward.

He reached out and caught me. His sure hands helped me to the seat. "Are you okay?"

Was I?

My briefs were wrapped around my right foot. He kneeled in front of me and unwound the white fabric from my ankle. Thank God my mother taught me about wearing clean underwear. Of course, she had mentioned auto accidents and hospitals. Not college professors and naked office sex.

Michael and I had sex.

And he loves me.

"Oh God."

Michael laughed. He reached for my face again, drawing me in for a long, slow kiss—like the first one we'd shared. When he released me, he pressed his forehead to mine. "I love you."

"Are you sure?"

He stared at me, his eyes searching mine. "I tried to tell myself for a long time I didn't have feelings for you. I think you and I have both known for a while now that what we have is special. I love my job, but I'm not going to deny what I feel for you. I'm not going to deny us any longer."

"They'll fire you?"

"I think I can convince the dean this isn't a scandalous thing, that I'm serious about you. I didn't realize I was going to have to convince you too. Good thing I already had this planned."

"Had what planned?" I slipped my toe through the pant leg of my briefs and twirled them in the air. "Sex on your desk?" I asked in the huskiest tone I could manage.

He laughed again.

So the trying-to-be-sexy thing wasn't for me.

His laugh ended, and he lunged at me, the kiss as passionate and full of strength and tongue and promise as any he'd given me when we had been on his desk.

Okay. So maybe my sex appeal was based in humor and not my ability to flirt with men's underwear.

"The sex was supposed to come later," he said. "After."

"After what?"

He went to his desk and used a key to unlock the top drawer. He pulled out a small box and brought it to me. A jewelry box. But not new. The top was worn; the black exterior faded. He kneeled beside me again and opened the lid. "After I gave you this."

A gold band.

"It was my father's. I'd love for you to wear it." He took my hand in his. "I'd love it if you'd marry me."

Damn. Where was that trash can? He either had to stop making me flustered as hell, or I had to quit the Cap'n Crunch. Could a grown man go cold turkey off the Cap'n?

The jewelry box and the wedding band inside trembled. He looked like he'd need the trash can before I did.

"Are you sure?" I asked again.

A smile spread over his lips, and the crinkles at the corners of his eyes returned. "You're the only person I've wanted since I met you. I'm not going to let our age difference or the fact that you're a student keep me out of your arms for one more day. I want to support you, comfort you, live with you, make love to you in a bed we share every night."

Okay. The Cap'n Crunch would have to go. I'd need protein mixed in.

He removed the ring from the box and held it out between us. "I want to spend my life with you."

It was my turn to grab for him. We ended up with him on my lap, his legs straddling my thighs, his groin pressed against my lower abdomen. Our tongues and bodies found a rhythm I didn't want to end.

But it had to end—I had something to say.

"Yes." I took his hand in mine, the ring pressed between our palms. "I'll marry you."

Something to Believe In

For all who are lost. May you find your way and know what it feels like to be loved.

A gust of snow pelted my face as I rounded the corner of the former Madison Street Elementary School. Raising the collar of my thin fleece coat, I hurried for the front door. The new sign hanging overhead read *Free Christmas Dinner.* That had me stopped in my tracks, and the tips of my sneakers dug into the snow that had been piling up on the sidewalk for the past several hours.

Christmas.

I'd seen the holiday decorations lining the streets and storefronts for weeks now, but I hadn't realized it was so close.

Christmas was the one time of year when I couldn't stop the memories.

"Sean Timothy Weber, if you walk out of here now and keep on being a disgusting little faggot, don't you ever bother coming back."

I shook off thoughts of her last words and moved for the shelter's front entrance again.

The man standing at the door smiled at me and held out a clear plastic bag containing a bar of soap, shaving cream, disposable razor, and condoms.

The essentials for most folks. Luxury items for guys like me.

"Merry Christmas," he said.

Reluctantly, because it meant taking my already freezing hand out of my pocket again, I accepted the bag and gave a nod of thanks. Another blast of icy snowfall smacked into me, practically knocking me off balance. Apparently I'd lost enough weight in the past few weeks, I couldn't hold my own against a little wind.

The guy with the plastic baggies of goodwill grabbed my arm and offered some support. When I was standing on steady feet again, he let go. "We're full up tonight, but come on inside and have something to eat. We've got a big spread, a real Christmas dinner."

I shivered as I forced the words out. "Today is C-C-Christmas?"

The out-of-place, ridiculously cheery grin faded from the man's face. He looked at me with the kind of pity I didn't get from too many people these days. You reach a certain point in both appearance and smell, and most folks pretend they don't notice you at all.

"It's Christmas Eve," he said.

That meant...*two years.*

Two years since I'd left home. The last four months of which I'd spent homeless and wandering the streets after I'd lost the job waiting tables, and my roommates had kicked me out when I couldn't make the rent.

I'd taken on any work I could find until I looked—and smelled—like a guy no one wanted to hire, not even for an under-the-table job hand-packaging DVDs of pirated porn. When the last of my money had run out and my stomach had felt like it was eating itself, I'd made the decision that had me retching my guts out as I'd bent over a stained toilet bowl.

It hadn't been a planned event. I'd been taking a leak in the bathroom near the historical fiction shelves at the main branch of the city public library when some guy in his forties wearing a sports jacket with frayed cuffs and carrying a briefcase that looked like he'd had it since day one out of college had stood at the urinal beside me. He'd pulled his dick out and whispered, "Twenty for a blow."

It had taken me a minute to get his meaning.

Twenty bucks.

I could have something real to eat.

After I'd answered with a nod, he'd tugged me to the stall at the end of the row behind us. When it was over and he'd left, I had stayed there bent over that toilet, clutching the twenty-dollar bill in my fist and dry-heaving for ten minutes.

No matter how bad that moment had been, the food and drink filling my belly a half hour later had convinced me I could do it again. And again. And again. Even with the knowledge that no one could survive forever the way I'd been living.

But I wanted to survive. I wanted to feel alive again.

The man with the clear bags of homeless holiday cheer held the door open for me. "Go on in, get warm, and have something to eat."

All I could manage was another nod. I went inside. The warmth of the still, dry air overwhelmed me with as much force as the icy, cold air had done outside.

Then the smells hit me. Turkey and ham and cookies fresh out of the oven. My mouth began watering, and I staggered through the entryway into the gym. If the faded murals on the walls were anything to go by, the building hadn't housed students since the 1990s. Thank God for people who demand their kids get a school without severely leaking roofs and archaic heating systems too costly to repair. Their castoffs gave me a place to sleep.

Well, some nights.

One side of the gym was filled with cots, the other with tables for chow time. At night, the tables came down and more cots went up. The guards also came out. Anyone caught fighting or stealing or shooting up or turning tricks was banned. No questions asked. You got one chance here.

Behind the men seated at the tables was a row of volunteers filling trays for more men shuffling by. I got in the line that wrapped around the perimeter of the gym and slipped the plastic bag with my lone Christmas gifts into my backpack.

Someone had gotten into the spirit and hung twinkling lights and strings of popcorn and cranberries over the backboard of each basketball hoop that was still suspended at the ends of the court. I hated to tell them, my fellow diners and I would've rather eaten the cranberries and popcorn than turn them into pointless garlands.

When it was my turn in line, I nodded my thanks at each person filling the sections of the plastic tray. I'd had meals at the Madison Street Men's Shelter before, but the size of this one smelled of a big donation from some corporation trying to buy free PR on the local news.

Well, actually, all I smelled was the food. Ham and green beans and mashed potatoes and gingerbread cookies. Although these cookies had no faces, not like my grandma had made when I was a kid. She'd always painted on their eyes and smiles, and hearts for buttons.

I carried my tray to a nearby table and squeezed in at an open space between two men. One was talking to each bite of food before he ate it, and the other smelled like he'd spent the past month sleeping in a dumpster overflowing with pickles.

I didn't care. I was long past the point of judging anyone. Hunched over the tray of steaming food, I wasn't sure where to start. So I shoveled in a bite of everything, working my way around the tray, not even waiting to swallow before adding in another forkful. I stuffed a big-ass bite of mashed potatoes slathered in gravy into my mouth and finally stopped to chew and swallow. I really needed to slow down or I'd get sick. I hadn't had this much food in my stomach in a long time.

Apparently, I didn't care about the post-meal vomiting. I crammed in another, bigger bite. Gravy squeezed out the corners of my mouth.

I suddenly felt self-conscious, which made no sense. At this point, I didn't care what the hell anyone thought of me.

With the mound of mashed potatoes still filling my mouth, I glanced up. Across the room was a guy around my age with deep brown hair. He was watching me from where he sat on the floor, leaning back against the wall riddled with holes from the bleachers that had been torn out of the gym. He had his tray of food on his lap, his long legs out straight in front of him, one black biker boot crossed over the other.

Biker Boots was still staring at me and smirking like he'd caught me jerking off.

I swallowed and swallowed again, and when the potatoes had finally finished making their way down my throat, I licked the gravy from the corners of my mouth.

He raised his eyebrows like I'd somehow impressed him. It was just mashed potatoes. What the hell was the big deal?

Biker Boots picked up his fork with an even bigger mound than I'd inhaled and held it up so I could be sure to see, then scooped the potatoes into his mouth and swallowed it all down in one try. He gestured like he'd just demonstrated the proper way to force down a giant gob of food at once.

Jerk. I flipped him off.

That time he laughed with a bigger smirk. Something told me he didn't do either all that often.

I went for the turkey next. He watched as I stacked several pieces on my fork, then opened wide. When I finished chewing and swallowing, Biker Boots followed my lead, balancing even more turkey on his fork.

With my next bite, we were both shoveling food into our mouths, racing to beat the other clearing his tray. I didn't let up until all I had left were the two dinner rolls. I picked up both and shoved them into my mouth. I had to look like a chipmunk hoarding nuts with the way my cheeks were puffed out.

Biker Boots shook his head, a full-on smile on his face now. He set his fork down, and when he finished chewing and swallowing, he gave a nod, then stood, picked up his coat, and headed to the gym's exit.

Disappointment hit my gut. An odd reaction. If there was one thing I'd learned living on the streets for the past couple of months, it was that guys like us didn't stick together, we didn't become friends or watch each other's backs.

I was on my own.

Slowly, I chewed the rolls and followed them down with a long guzzle of milk. That tiny carton of milk, the lunch tray, the gym…it all made me feel like a child. Small. Inconsequential.

As I chugged back the last of the milk, I couldn't help but catch sight of the twinkling lights on the backboard above me— one of the few signs in the room that it was Christmas. I stared at one blinking green bulb and let myself remember. The fake tree that had been put up year after year with its missing branches and gaping holes where you could see right through to the wall behind it. The presents with my name that were always under that tree the week leading up to Christmas. The mistletoe Grandpa would carry in his pocket and hold over Grandma's head every chance he got.

Those memories didn't last long. They never did.

Another replaced them.

"If you walk out of here now and keep on being a disgusting little faggot, don't you ever bother coming back."

Those were the last words I'd heard my mom shout as I ran out the door, a backpack slung over my shoulder, crammed full with my favorite pair of jeans, the demolition derby sweatshirt I'd won at the county fair that year, and my laptop—because I'd had no idea how hard life for a high school dropout was going to be and I'd foolishly thought I'd have time and money for gaming, movies, and music. Instead, I'd ended up selling the laptop for rent money. When I'd left home, I hadn't really given my actions a lot of thought. I couldn't get out of that house— that town—fast enough. My skin was still crawling from the perverted counselor's hand sliding inside the front of my jeans.

He was supposed to "fix me," she'd said.

Someone needed to fix him. Permanently.

Funny how I'd run away from that and ended up with old men touching me anyway. At least these men paid me for the privilege.

I didn't even try to turn that counselor in or tell anyone other than my mom what he'd done. That was my biggest regret. Instead of stopping him, I'd run from him, from the high school diploma I would've received six months later, and from those last words my mom had shrieked at my back.

She'd laugh her ass off if she saw where I'd ended up.

The man beside me smacked my arm. "Do you see that?" He pointed to the ham on his tray. "They are feeding us baked children."

As I got up from the table, I said, "No, man, there's no kids allowed in here."

He looked disappointed. I left him to it and crossed the room to clear my tray. No stopping the inevitable. They didn't have a bed for me. Time to stake my claim somewhere.

I exited the shelter and raised the collar on my coat again. There was no sign the snow planned on stopping its assault on the city. I rounded the corner to the alley. I really should've been heading to the highway overpass north of the shelter. Someone usually had a fire going. I'd been sleeping there more than anywhere else in the past several weeks, but I couldn't force myself to walk that far, not with the full stomach and how hard the snow was barreling down. I'd just have to find a doorway to hunch in for a few hours. One of those shops farther down on Madison usually worked. The cops didn't tour that area much and the shops were too small to bother with much security.

I stopped halfway down the alley where the buildings on each side blocked much of the falling snow and wind.

Someone moved in the shadows beside a dumpster. A man stepped into the dim glow from the streetlights just as my eyes adjusted to the darkness behind him where a door was open. A kid not much more than sixteen lay on a couch inside the apartment. His head was propped on the arm of the couch, his eyes rolled back. Another, even younger kid was on the other end, sitting up, a needle in his hand.

For once, I didn't turn away and take off. I leaned against the brick wall and watched that young man's face soften as the pain and misery faded away.

The guy who'd walked out of the open door had stopped. "You looking for something?"

I just kept on staring at the kid on the couch.

This wasn't me.

I was just so cold and tired. The high of the warm food filling my belly hadn't lasted long. I wanted to forget that I was alone for another Christmas, forget what I'd been doing to survive, and most importantly, forget the memories that stupid string of Christmas lights had brought out.

Just for a little while.

"Come on. You deserve some relief." He tilted his head to the room behind him where the others lay on that couch completely unaware of the snow blowing in through the open door. "I'll show you how," he added.

"Don't." Biker Boots was walking toward us from the end of the alley. He was staring me down as he'd done when I'd first seen him in the shelter. He was taller and broader than he'd looked earlier. He had a strong, solid appearance despite his lean frame. Although, that could've had something to do with the determination in his stride as he advanced. "Don't do it," he said, his gaze still locked on mine.

"Fuck off," the other guy said. He'd taken a step away but wasn't backing off completely.

Biker Boots gestured toward the street. "Let's get out of here."

I didn't think. I just nodded and followed him down the alley.

When I'd lost my apartment and had spent the first night wandering the city streets, I'd made myself a few promises. The first…no matter how bad it got, I'd never give in and get fucked up.

Now, four months in and I'd almost done it.

We neared the end of the alley, and my new friend—if I dared call him that—didn't even stop, just kept on moving along the sidewalk until another guy stepped into my path.

"Hey, cutie."

Biker Boots came to my side. "Don't." Apparently, his favorite word. He grabbed my arm and dragged me with him, trudging forward faster than before. When we reached the next block, he finally let go.

I stopped to catch my breath. "What'd you do that for? I might've gotten enough for a room. It's practically a fucking blizzard out here or haven't you noticed?"

One side of his mouth lifted in an amused smirk. "You would've been spending the night someplace warm, that's for sure. He's a cop. And not one that wants a free blow and will let you go."

I jerked around to look back the way we'd come. I'd almost gotten my ass thrown in jail for the first time.

Merry Fucking Christmas.

Biker Boots tilted his head in the opposite direction. "Come on. I know a place." He continued walking at a quick pace, his hands shoved into his pockets, and I followed.

The abandoned warehouse sat along the docks. With the river so close, the wind was even colder, the snow now coming down harder. Inside, the building was divided into several large rooms. Men and women were lying on the floor everywhere. A child cried near an open window, and the smell of urine and rank body odor filled the air. We headed up a flight of stairs and walked past several rooms that looked like they'd been offices at one time. We entered the last room on the left. There was no door, no furniture. Just a couple of empty crates and a thin mattress, so small it had to be for a little kid's bed. A man with a full beard lay on his side on the mattress and three others were curled up at other spots on the floor. They didn't stir as we stepped inside. The room wasn't warm by any stretch of the word, but we were out of the snow and wind and that alone was a real gift, more than the baggie of soap and shaving cream.

Biker Boots didn't say anything. Just pointed to the far corner with an empty space behind two crates. He pried back a loose board on the floor and pulled out a sweatshirt. He tossed it to me, then took out another he wadded up into a ball and used as a pillow. He lay flat on his back staring up at the ceiling.

I lowered myself to the floor and lay on my side, watching him for a while. I was just starting to relax, to think about closing my eyes when he spoke, his gaze still locked on the ceiling like he was talking to it instead of me.

"It can get kinda rough here when it's this crowded. Some guys'll do anything for a fix. Or a fuck."

So much for relaxing. I'd managed not to get beaten or raped for the past four months. I sure wanted to keep that record going.

He spoke again in that calm, low voice he'd said everything with. "We could take turns sleeping."

"Okay."

"You first." He sat up and leaned against the wall behind him, his arms folded over his chest, his long legs crossed at the boot-clad ankles as he watched the open doorway across the room.

"Thanks." I closed my eyes. I wasn't sure why I trusted him, but I did.

"What's your name?"

I opened my eyes at his whispered words. He was still staring at the doorway.

"Sean. Yours?"

I didn't think he was going to answer. Then he finally said, "Gavin."

And with that one name, I was no longer alone.

* * * *

Almost a year later…

"Disgusting little faggot."

I shifted on the cold tile floor, searching for a spot on my kneecaps that didn't already feel sore as hell, and tried to shut down that voice inside my head repeating those hateful words from three years ago.

"Don't you ever bother coming back."

Even after all this time, they were the same words that seeped into my mind whenever I found myself on my knees in a public men's room.

The man standing over me grunted, and I finally sank into that space between reality and illusion where I always let myself go in moments like these, as if I were witnessing another guy do the things I did in those restrooms, parked cars, and adult bookstore basements.

I wasn't the one selling myself for money. It was someone else.

Guys who carried a 4.0 GPA through three years of high school didn't end up on their knees with a stranger's cock shoved to the back of their throats for some cash. They worked hard and studied and went to college. They got jobs that offered retirement plans and dental benefits and whatever other shit people who didn't live on the streets considered important.

The man above me let out another grunt, and I barely heard

it that time. I was too far away, suspended in that space between that bathroom stall and anywhere else. Where I couldn't hear my mom's words. Where I was warm and fed and doing something mundane and foreign to me now, like reading a book or playing a video game. Where Gavin's touch was the only one I knew. Where I made love with him every night in our own bed, our own home.

Even if that last bit was a fantasy that might never come true, the rest would soon.

If I could just float above that homeless guy on his knees who looked like me a little longer.

Then the moment changed. The stranger pulled his dick out of my mouth and started jerking off. The illusion was broken. Shattered.

It wasn't some other guy in that men's room. I was the one on the floor, my knees digging into the stained gray tile, a puddle of some guy's piss beside me, a stranger's hand fisted in my hair, my head yanked back as I waited for him to finish so I could grab the cash and get the hell out of there.

Just fucking come already.

The small bathroom stall filled with the slick sound of his hand moving over the moist skin of his dick I'd just had crammed into my mouth. I reached into my coat pocket and clutched the folded up piece of paper, holding on to it like it was all that would keep me from floating away completely and never being me again. I closed my eyes and tried to let the sound of that hand caressing flesh fade from my reality.

No such luck.

I let up on my grip, not wanting to rip the paper in my pocket before I could show Gavin later.

Such a fragile thing, paper, and yet this one held the key to everything. At least for me. Because printed across the top was my name.

After two years barely scraping by on whatever jobs a high school dropout could get and more than another year selling myself on the streets, I was on my way out of this life. And I was taking Gavin with me.

Another groan, and a spurt of the man's release hit my

cheek. He jerked my head back farther. More splashed onto my chin and my other cheek.

"Fuck yeah." Those grunted words were said in appreciation for his own efforts, not mine.

The odd silence that followed made it seem like nothing had happened in that bathroom stall.

A dream. A nightmare.

The man standing over me closed his pants and threw two bills at my face where they stuck to his cum for a second. No hesitation. He took off, and the stall door banged shut behind me. When the outer door of the bathroom followed suit, I got off my knees and exited the stall. Stopping at the row of sinks, I rinsed out my mouth and scrubbed the evidence of what I'd just done from my face. My hands shook as I ran my fingers through my hair. All this time, and I never could stop that reaction when it was over.

I clutched the edge of the sink in both hands and bent forward. The rank stench of shit and cum filled my next breath, and I swallowed down the gag. Using a paper towel, I dried the cum from the cash and washed my hands again. I gave another attempt at smoothing the unruly dark hair. I hated the fucking curls, but haircuts weren't high on my priority list.

The facial hair made me look five years older, which I both liked and hated. I didn't get as many tricks when I didn't shave. Everyone loved young dick.

Well, practically everyone I'd ever met.

I'd need to get cleaned up before I could do what the social worker at the shelter had said came next. A shave. Haircut. New clothes. I'd have to transform into someone presentable. Become my old self?

I stared at the pale, dirt-streaked face in the mirror, the moist, swollen lips, the blank eyes looking back at me.

Nope, the young man I had been was long gone.

Wiping my mouth with the frayed sleeve of my coat, I left the bathroom and glanced at the clock over the ticket windows.

I wasn't sure if the time Gavin had yelled out the car's window as they'd pulled away seven days ago was an estimate or not, but I wasn't about to be anywhere else, even if I had to wait all night.

A cop rounded the corner that led to the bus station's security office. He paused and got a good look at me. I wasn't there to catch a bus, and we both knew he got that as he headed my way. I took off and didn't let up until I exited the alleyway four blocks from the bus station. I raced around a pile of snow the city plows had dumped at the end of the alley and jerked to a stop in front of the coffee shop, all the while scanning the packed crowd on the sidewalk and the traffic crawling through the intersection.

No sign of Gavin or the car he'd left in.

I made my way through the crowd pushing past me and went to the street vendor working the corner, steam rising up from his open cart until he caught sight of me and slammed the lid shut. I ordered two loaded hot dogs. He gave me a look that said he wasn't touching the dogs until I showed him the cash. He'd been around long enough to know better. So had I. To him I looked like exactly what I was.

Homeless. No job. No cash. No future.

Just a guy with a mouth that was made for sucking. That's what one of my cop tricks Mitch always said. He never could resist testing that theory whenever he spotted me during his shift. At least he paid me.

I handed over the money and was awarded my first bite of anything to eat in two days. Scarfing down the dogs, I eased my way through the crowd to stand near the brick wall of the coffee shop and tried to blend into the background. That corner was one of our favorite places, which was why he'd chosen there to meet. When we stood on that sidewalk, talking, laughing, we could pretend we were just two normal guys, a part of the crowd of shoppers, not one more thing that could be bought and paid for, and not like we were waiting until it was dark so we could head to River View Park or Sycamore Street with its line of adult bookstores where we'd do whatever we had to do for a few more bucks.

Five minutes went by, the dogs long gone, and I was still alone, waiting.

I tried to ignore the never-ending chime of the bell from the volunteer soliciting donations in front of the coffee shop. Christmas carols poured out from speakers outside the department store across the street. So loud there was no way I could pretend I didn't hear that odd mix of overly cheery and depressing songs.

All those men and women, carrying their shopping bags overflowing with packages and buying their tiny coffees that cost more than I'd ever pay for something that didn't include an entire chicken dinner on the side, amazed me.

Didn't they see me? Didn't they get how some of us lived?

Or maybe they did, and that's why a few didn't just stride by that little red bucket and the bell-ringing man in the Santa hat. Maybe that's why they slowed enough to flick in a few coins or bills. To ease their conscience before they stuffed themselves with Christmas dinner and all the trimmings, before they opened a shitload of gifts they didn't need or want, before they spent the day singing carols and spent the night making love to someone special they'd kissed under the mistletoe.

I laughed. A week ago we'd stood at that same corner, and when Gavin had seen me watching people walk by, he'd said, *"Fuck them. Fuck Christmas. And fuck that bell, that bucket full of guilt, and their happy, safe lives."*

He had a thing about not taking a handout, and he never asked anyone for help. That night we'd met at the shelter had been one of the rare times he'd come inside. Since then, I had to be very specific with him about how cold and tired I was to get him to consider taking two cots at the shelter. And he never accepted any of the donated clothes or hygiene products. He'd rather suck an extra cock to buy a coat or pack of condoms. I'd done my best to try to convince him taking a free damn condom didn't make him weak, but I hadn't been successful yet.

I shifted on my feet where I waited by the brick wall. A half hour crawled by. Then another.

The falling snow swirled around my ankles, and a gust blew the whirl of wet flakes into my face. My gut chose right then to make that gurgling sound I'd grown accustomed to over the past year. Like a monster from one of those alien movies was trying to claw its way out, even with the two dogs I'd just fed it. My knees still stung from where they'd been pressing into the tiled bathroom floor and my jaw ached. The fucker hadn't bothered to tell me he couldn't come from a blowjob, just let me go on and on.

Despite all that, a smile hit my lips and time no longer mattered. Neither did the cum I could practically still feel on my face, or anything else I'd done in the past seven days. I could breathe again without the constant ache in my chest.

The black SUV with gold trim he'd left in had pulled up to the curb.

I let out a long exhale and leaned back against the brick wall.

I couldn't tear my gaze away from that black SUV. I imagined him strolling toward me, tossing back the bangs of that brown hair with a tip of his head, those green eyes focused on me, along with the rare smile he never shared with anyone else.

A part of me hadn't really believed I'd see him again.

Offers like the one he'd gotten to spend a week at a house in the country with some old fart for the kind of cash the man had promised didn't happen for guys like us. Not where you didn't end up dead before the week was up. That shit was for the movies.

Not that movies were a part of my everyday life. I'd seen a ton of movie posters on the sides of buses and buildings, even caught a bunch of trailers in the motel room Mitch always took me to. He liked to leave the preview channel on. Maybe so he wouldn't have to lie when his wife asked what he'd done on his break that day. But a real movie? The last one I could remember was a superhero flick I'd gone to three years earlier with my grandpa.

Another lifetime ago.

The door on the black SUV opened and out came the passenger's right leg. He slid halfway out of the car and stopped so only his ass and legs were visible. It didn't matter. I had all the proof I needed. I'd spent the last year dreaming of that body.

A week ago, when he'd made his decision and I'd watched him climb into that SUV, I had panicked, wanting to haul him back out the minute the door shut. I had wanted to do anything I could to get him to stop, but I knew he'd never change his mind. No one turned down that kind of money. Even if there was a chance he'd end up floating face down in the river and become some cautionary tale I'd hear one guy telling another at the shelter on Madison late at night as we lay on our cots, each of us under a thin blanket, our shoes still on our feet because no one took their shoes off, even at the shelter. You might as well toss them to the first guy you passed by with bare feet or holes in the soles of his pair.

I couldn't stop staring at those scuffed black boots paused on the curb before me, and the long legs that led into the car where he was probably collecting the rest of the cash.

Gavin was alive.

I wanted to sprint across the sidewalk and drag him out of that car, money or no money. How crazy was that? He'd already done whatever the old guy wanted, and we needed the cash.

Despite that, I was about to rush toward him when he finally stood, stuffing an unbelievably large wad of dough in the front pocket of his jeans. Gavin scanned the crowd of pedestrians scurrying by on the sidewalk as the SUV took off behind him. He spotted me, and he didn't hesitate. With a tilt of his head as he approached, he flipped the hair off his forehead and threw me that smile. "Hey."

And just like that, life was bearable again. The shitty fucking blowjob from earlier, the guy's cum on my skin, and the feel of those two sweaty, crumpled bills sticking to me were gone.

Those green eyes and that smile never failed to make the reality of my life fade away. No one but him made the dark, frigid nights not so long or so lonely, or made me laugh. Before him, I'd forgotten how good it felt to laugh, to feel anything.

"Sean." He snapped his fingers in front of my face. "You okay?"

"Yeah." Biggest understatement of my life.

He laughed. "Damn, I missed you, kid."

I never got why he called me *kid*. He was a year younger. Over half a foot taller, tougher, broader, but definitely younger.

Wait…

He missed me?

Why did he say shit like that? I didn't want him to play me.

He had to know how I felt about him. Even if we'd never done much more than sleep touching along our lengths for the extra body heat, he had to know I was fucking in love every time I looked at him.

"Did you get it?" he asked.

I nodded, feeling the sting of tears I never let anyone see but him, and he'd only caught them once: after a guy had gotten rough with me, held me down, and fucked me without a condom, which led us to the free clinic for more frequent testing than we'd bothered with before.

I pulled the paper from my pocket. "I got it yesterday."

He took the paper, holding it like that one sheet was more precious than the money he'd just earned. "I knew you could do it." He examined the words and didn't let on what we both knew. He couldn't read most of what it said. "Damn proud of you, kid."

"Thanks." I ducked my head. Of all the people I'd known in my life, I wanted to impress him more than anyone. "You'll have yours soon too."

He handed back the paper and scoffed, kicking at an empty disposable coffee cup on the sidewalk with the toe of his boot. The reaction pissed me off. He was wicked smart. So reading and writing came harder to him than kids half his age. That didn't mean he couldn't pass the high school equivalency exam one day. Then he'd have the same GED certificate as the one I'd just shown him, but with his name across the top. Preparing for the test would just take him a little longer. He'd get there eventually. If he stopped running off for a week at a time.

I studied him. He looked good. Clean and shaved and fed, not a scratch on him. "Are *you* okay?"

"Yeah." He kicked the cup once more, and it flew off the sidewalk onto the street. "Was a sweet deal. Gave me more than he'd promised."

"More? Jesus."

Gavin nodded and leaned against the wall beside me. "And I have an idea." The smile was back. How could he spend a week with some old fucker touching him, making him do God-only-knows what, and still smile like that? "Let's get a room. A real hotel room. Soak in a hot bath. Watch stupid-ass movies. Eat until we explode."

"Oh God, that sounds good."

"Stay there until after Christmas."

Christmas? That was a week away. How much cash did he shove in his pocket? "What the hell did he make you do?"

The smile fled from Gavin's face. That stoic, I-take-no-shit-from-anyone-and-don't-give-a-fuck-if-I-live-or-die   expression he usually wore around everyone else slid into place. He shrugged. "Kinky shit."

I opened my mouth to ask more but clamped it shut. We didn't talk about it. Ever.

"Sorry," I mumbled, but I couldn't keep from imagining what kinds of twisted stuff the gray-haired old man had made him do. The guy had to have been almost seventy. My heart ached more with each picture that rushed through my mind.

Gavin shrugged again. "Got enough for a week and then some if we get a cheap place. A warm bed, a shower. We'll order pizza. You in?" There was something off about him, like he was trying to be nonchalant about this, but he wasn't exactly pulling it off.

I hadn't known him to try at anything. He just was who he was and made no apologies for it.

"Hey, you two!" The guy who managed the coffee shop glared at us from the open doorway, waving an arm through the air. "Get the hell out of here or I'm calling the cops." It wasn't an empty threat. He'd done it before.

Gavin yelled over his shoulder, "Fuck off. It's a free country." He held on to my arm and tugged me with him around the corner of the building. We'd only made it halfway down the alley when he pulled us to a stop and asked, "What?"

I'd been shaking my head since we'd taken off. "We should make it last longer."

"Sean, money never lasts. You know that." He paused, considered me. His face had taken on a new expression I'd never seen from him. Something tired and lost. He stared off toward the street. "I want a memory that'll last."

I wasn't sure what he meant by that. "Okay. If you're sure."

He still wouldn't look my way. "I'm sure."

I reached into my pocket and pulled out the rest of the cash I'd earned. "Here. It's not much."

"Where'd you get all that? You were supposed to eat while I was gone."

"I did. I just… there was this new kid at the park. Barely a teenager."

Gavin closed his eyes and a tense sigh escaped from between his lips.

"He would've froze without a coat."

"So you gave him our money and then you…"

I nodded.

"You promised—" He stared off down the alley again and swallowed hard. The disappointment on his face was impossible to ignore.

Before he'd left, he'd made me swear I wouldn't hustle until he got back. Which I didn't get. After all this time, why would he ask that of me now?

Unless…

My breath caught in my chest.

Did it make him as sick as it made me to think of someone using him like that? Someone touching him? Someone doing the things I wanted to do with him?

For the past few weeks, he'd been the one to go off and get us some cash whenever we were low. He'd come back to the abandoned warehouse or the alley by the shelter or wherever we were "staying" for a few days, carrying food and bottles of water. Then, when we ran out, he'd sneak off again while I slept like he was trying to protect me from what I'd been doing since before I'd met him.

Gavin shook his head. "Doesn't matter now. Where to?"

"There's a motel not far from the shelter. It's cheap but not bad, kinda nice." I paused, kept my head down. "Mitch always takes me there."

"No." Gavin stood taller. "Nowhere we've been like that."

"Okay," I said. "You ever been to that hotel on Summit a couple blocks north of the shelter? Might be more expensive but should have a TV and plenty of hot water."

He smiled and started for the end of the alley. "Let's go."

I followed. "Now?"

"Right now. Before someone has a chance to jump us for the cash." He exited onto the sidewalk, hands shoved in the pockets of his jeans. I followed, trying hard not to let my thoughts wander too far into the possibility of what the next week would bring.

Or why he wanted this so badly.

* * * *

"Here, you first." Gavin handed me one of the bags with the clothes and other supplies we'd purchased at the discount store on our way to the hotel. We'd gotten enough junk food and some healthier shit to last longer than a week. He'd said he didn't want to leave the room once we got there.

In the hotel bathroom, I brushed my teeth, showered, and shaved, wishing we'd splurged on something I could buzz my hair with. At least I'd thought to get a pair of scissors so I could chop the fucking curls off. I'd wait on that for later. I didn't want to hold up Gavin any longer. He'd want to scrub away the week he'd just had—not that it could be washed away that easily.

We traded places, and I decided to do something I hadn't done in a long time: unpack our shit like we we're staying there indefinitely and wouldn't have to take off at a moment's notice. After all, they couldn't kick us out. We'd pre-paid for the week.

The tiny room didn't have much. One double bed with what looked like half dead weeds growing all over the red bedspread and a TV that sat on a lone dresser at the foot of the bed. The wall over the headboard had a disturbing painting of a pond with a pack of Labrador Retrievers chasing down a flock of ducks. Half the ducks were already in the air, wings flapping as they fled for their lives. Most of the dogs were barking like mad. One had the limp body of a duck clenched in his jaw.

I didn't care about those about-to-be dead birds or anything else in the place. The room was all ours until Christmas.

If only I had the money to show Gavin what the holiday could really be like. With a tree and gifts and lights and cheesy Rudolph and Frosty the Snowman decorations. What it had been like when I'd spent every Christmas Eve at my grandparents' house growing up, and what it had never been like for Gavin.

He'd spent most of his childhood in and out of foster homes after his mom had OD'd when he'd been five, and by the time I'd met him, he trusted no one and had never known what it was to be loved. That was why he amazed me. Despite all he'd been through, he hadn't started using or ended up in prison—or dead—and for some reason, he'd reached out to me as we'd eaten the free holiday meal at the shelter that night we'd met. He'd watched me from across the room, and instead of walking away as soon as I'd made eye contact with him, like he'd done with everyone else, he'd connected with me in his own way. Probably the only way he could in that moment.

In the weeks that followed, somehow I'd gotten him to trust me.

And someday I'd get to show him everything he'd missed out on in his youth. A real Christmas. A real home.

I stashed the extra clothes in the bottom drawer of the dresser, then dumped the food and other supplies into the top two drawers. I tried not to focus on the boxes of condoms and lube that tumbled out of the last bag.

Gavin had always been adamant about spending some of any money we had on condoms. I didn't want to think about how we'd need those again in a week.

I slammed the dresser drawer shut, and for once I skipped putting on my shoes and instead went with only a new pair of socks. I tried out the bed, lying on my side and snuggling into the pillow. My hair was still damp, but for the first time in over a year, I felt warm in the middle of winter. I couldn't remember when I'd last been in a real bed where I wasn't getting paid for it.

I awoke some time later. The bedspread had been folded over on top of me. Gavin was sitting at the foot of the bed, fully dressed in a new pair of jeans and the blue Superman T-shirt he'd found on the discount rack. I wasn't sure how long I'd been asleep. His hair was dry, yet the scent of the coconut from the cheap soap we'd bought still lingered in the air. It gave the room a summertime feel that didn't fit the winter storm outside. He was leaning forward, his elbows on his knees, his hands clasped before him. He had his head hanging low, and his broad shoulders held more tension than I'd seen in a long time.

I threw back the blanket and scrambled to a sitting position. "What's wrong?"

He slowly lifted his head. The tension seemed to ratchet up another notch as he made eye contact with me over his shoulder. "Nothing. Let's order food."

I gave a nod that he missed since he'd already taken off for the phone on the dresser.

Nothing, my ass. There was something eating away at him.

I watched him for a minute, but he didn't say anything else. I was always wanting him to say more, watching and waiting for the words or emotions that rarely came. Why'd I have to fall for the strong, silent type?

I guess it wasn't just him who held back. We'd both learned to bury our feelings.

And maybe that's what was wrong. He'd been holding on to something for too long now.

* * * *

"Oh God." Gavin rolled onto his back on the bed. "My stomach's gonna bust." He lifted his T-shirt and laid a palm over his abs like that one light touch would keep him from exploding.

I ate another bite of the last piece of pizza, my gaze locked on the expanse of skin between his shirt and the low-riding jeans. I didn't get to see him when he wasn't fully clothed nearly often enough. Despite feeling as stuffed as Gavin sounded, I shoved another bite into my mouth, anything to keep from leaning forward and kissing all that warm, clean skin, breathing in his scent—with no trace of some other guy.

I dropped the rest of the piece of pizza into the box on the bed between us and moved around to lie facing him. "We're gonna get spoiled staying here."

He gave me a long, conflicted look, like he wanted to bring something up but wasn't sure how or where to start. Then he broke the stare and sat up in a rush. "Wanna watch a movie? Something with big-ass guns and shit blowing up?"

I nodded. I wanted to ask him what his deal was, but something told me not yet, that whatever it was about, I couldn't push him on it. Not that I had any experience getting someone to talk about anything other than what they wanted me to do for fifty bucks.

I sat up and leaned back against the headboard. "I haven't seen a movie in forever."

He grabbed the remote off the dresser and dropped to the end of the bed. He flipped through channels as he asked, "Did you go out a lot back home? To movies and shit?"

I paused with the empty pizza box in mid-air. We never talked about home. All I knew of Gavin's past in the foster care system was that he'd taken off when the last foster dad had decided his fists were the best way to get Gavin to "stay in line."

I set the box on the floor beside the bed. "I used to go to the movies with my grandpa. He'd take my cousins and me almost every week."

"That's cool." Gavin kept searching channels. He stopped on a cooking show, some old guy in a chef's hat talking in a near whisper about placing a lobster into a freezer for a few minutes before plunging it into the hot water. The most humane method for boiling the creature to its death since it would be numb first and would also help reduce the twitching of the lobster's tail as it died.

I'd been that cold—and afraid—far too often in my short life. I think I'd rather they kill me first before the torture of the slow freeze-and-boil routine. I made a silent promise to myself. No matter how much money I ever had in my life, I'd never fucking eat lobster.

"He was nice to you?" Gavin asked.

"Grandpa? Yeah."

Maybe it was the normalcy of a full stomach and being clean, watching TV in a hotel room, or maybe it was that I'd always wanted us to be like this together—sharing all of ourselves. In either case, I kept on talking. "There was this theater in town, only had one screen, but they showed a different movie every week. He'd take us on Saturdays after he finished in his garden. He always smelled like wet dirt and this organic fish fertilizer he used on his plants, so my asshole cousins never wanted to sit by him. But I didn't mind." I ran my hand through my hair, wishing the memories wouldn't come back so easily. "I liked it best when it was just him and me anyway."

We'd seen every superhero movie released since I was in the first grade, and we'd watched a ton of the classics he had on DVD too. How many of those Saturday movies had I missed since I'd been gone?

Gavin hit mute on the TV, tossed the remote aside. "Where'd you grow up?"

"Just a dinky little town. It's nowhere special."

He lowered to the bed on his side, his head propped in his hand. Something about that action and the quiet stillness of the room around us gave the moment a different feel from any other we'd spent together.

More private.

More real.

Which was odd. Sometimes I'd felt completely alone with him when we were surrounded by men at the shelter.

Or at least, I'd thought that's how I'd felt. Maybe I'd never been alone with the real Gavin. The one who was watching me now.

He reached out and laid a hand on my right thigh. "You came from there, so yeah, it is special." He paused as if he wanted to make sure I got his meaning.

I wasn't sure I did.

"In Ohio, right?" he asked. He rubbed my thigh, his hand so warm I could feel it through my jeans. The only time he'd touched me even close to the same way had been about warming me up after I'd trudged through the snow to the warehouse from the park in a worse snowstorm nearly a year ago. That touching had been clinical. Or at least I'd tried to pretend it had so my heart wouldn't be crushed when he rolled over to go to sleep.

I nodded, my next words catching in my throat. I swallowed and tried again. "Angola, Ohio. This time of year, every house and all the shops lining Main Street are decked out in Christmas lights. There are giant stars on the telephone poles and reindeer pulling a sleigh in the town square. Like someplace you'd see on a postcard."

"Pretty?"

"I guess. More like it has this quiet, polite normalcy. But you have to look close to see the real place. I mean, the kinds of people who actually live there." I pulled at a loose green thread on the bedspread beside me. The thread kept on unraveling. Maybe I could pull all those ugly weeds out and leave behind something plain but more beautiful. "The people—they're not so pretty."

His hand stopped moving. "Like your parents?"

"Yeah."

"Did you ever tell them or your grandparents you were gay?"

I gave up on the weed whacking and crossed my arms over my chest. "Thought we were gonna catch a movie?"

"Right." He removed his hand from my leg, and I immediately regretted my words as he returned to the end of the bed and reached for the remote. He pointed it at the TV but paused before clicking on the sound, his back to me. "You are, though, right?"

"What?"

"Gay."

"Me?" I choked out a laugh. Was he serious?

Apparently so. He clutched the remote like it was a grenade, and if he let go, the room—and the two of us—would explode into a thousand pieces. I wasn't sure he was even breathing.

"Oh, God yeah," I said. "I'm gay. It's why I left home."

He sighed and eased up on the remote. He started changing channels again, stopping when he hit some action, one of those low-tech time-travel movies with the former governor from California.

Gavin kept the sound muted, and the time-traveling cyborg guy didn't seem as threatening without the sounds of his guns going off. It's amazing what silence will do to a moment.

"Gavin?"

Slowly, he looked back at me over his shoulder.

"Are you?" I asked.

His mouth turned up at the corners. "Yeah, I'm gay."

A wave of relief overcame me. I felt dizzy, like a weight had been torn away from my chest in an instant. I hadn't even realized I'd been worried about Gavin's sexual orientation, but maybe I should've. There were plenty of guys hustling who'd never touch another man's dick if they weren't desperate for their next fix.

"Sean, I..." Gavin paused. "I don't want you to..." He turned away again, and the silence stretched on.

"What?"

"You'll get a job soon. Then you can apply for one of those low income apartments that social worker talked about."

That was the plan.

"You'll be done with this life." Gavin had never doubted I'd find a way out of the trap so many of us got stuck in.

"We both will," I said.

We had been determined to stay off drugs, to find our way to a better life.

Or maybe that last part was just me. I always got the feeling he never expected he'd live past twenty-five.

Gavin shook his head so long I wasn't sure he'd stop. "I'm not as smart as you."

"Fuck that. You're smarter."

He threw me a grateful look, then asked, "You ever notice how that social worker talks to you and ignores me? She knows you have what it takes. Not me."

"Who cares what she thinks. You have what it takes too."

He went back to examining the floor before his feet, his elbows on his knees.

I moved to sit beside him. "Gavin—"

He reached up and patted the top of my head. "Your hair's sticking up all over."

"It was wet when I fell asleep." I really didn't care. Not with the way he kept on smoothing my hair with his palm. His warm hand settled at the back of my neck, and I closed my eyes. "I can't wait to cut it." Although, with the way he'd stroked my hair like he'd never felt something so alluring, maybe cutting it off wasn't such a good idea anymore.

"Don't." He brushed a lock from my forehead with the pad of his thumb. I trembled with that one touch. "I like it like this," he added.

"I look like a girl."

"Trust me"—he kept on running his fingers through the hair above my ear—"you don't look like a girl."

"But they always—"

"What?"

I squeezed my eyes shut again. Why did I keep talking about it? "They like grabbing on to it when I'm—"

Gavin dropped his hand and shot off the bed. "We got scissors, right?"

"Yeah," I pointed to the dresser. "They're in the top drawer."

He got them and went into the bathroom for a comb, his body moving with the determination I'd found sexy since the first night he'd headed my way in that alley when I'd been about to make the biggest mistake of my life.

Or maybe it was what he was up to now that moved me.

He came back to stand by the bed. "Do you mind if I do it?"

"Not at all. Chop away." I could barely wait another minute to have the curls gone.

Apparently, he couldn't either. He laid a towel behind me on the bed and picked up the comb and scissors. "How short?"

"As short as you can but don't make me look like a freak."

He laughed. "Not possible." He combed and snipped away.

I squirmed as loose strands tickled the top of my ears, and he laughed again.

"Sit still." Then he grew serious as he worked in silence for a while. His next words were whispered more to the falling hair than to me. "I can't stand that you've had to live like this." He was very still, the comb clenched in one hand, the scissors in the other.

The room fell silent once again. I craned my neck to get a look at his face. I couldn't read the expression. I reached for the hand with the scissors and held it in mine. "I feel the same about you."

He gave a nod and went back to the haircut. A few snips later, he paused, a section of my hair between his fingers. "Did you tell your grandparents?"

It took me a second to get the shift in conversation. "That I'm gay?"

"Yeah." *Snip. Snip.* He moved around to my other side.

"No. But I'm sure my mom did after I left." I paused, picked at the bedspread beside me some more. "They were real religious. Like my parents. And they adored my mom. I wasn't sure what they'd think, so I never said anything. They were quiet people, didn't talk about much. Just went to church and worked in their garden."

"And took you to the movies. Maybe they would've been okay about it."

"I just…" I shrugged and shifted on my ass. "I couldn't stand the thought of finding out they hated me too."

He nodded. *Snip. Snip.* A curl fell onto my lap, and I resisted the urge to swipe it away like it had caught fire.

"Did you get along with anyone else?" he asked. "Friends at school?" He never asked so many questions. He never talked this much at all.

"I had a few friends, just not anyone that mattered. But I did have this one teacher I really liked. And her husband was cool. He was my boss at the grocery store."

Gavin laughed. "You bagged groceries?"

"Yeah. Why's that funny?"

"Just sounds like something you'd see on TV. Didn't think people really did shit like that." He tilted my head forward so he could get to the hair at the base of my neck. "I bet you were a nerd in school too."

My mouth dropped open. "Was not!"

I was, but for some reason I didn't want him seeing me that way. He was probably one of those kids who defied labels. Or at least was the kind of guy no one in school wanted to label for fear he'd beat the shit out of them.

He laughed again and stepped back. "All done. It's kinda spiky, but it's definitely short."

I stood and went to the bathroom mirror. I couldn't hold back the emotion. Tears filled my eyes as I stared at the new me. My hair looked darker. And I looked older. A man. I shook my head. "I don't know what's wrong with me."

"I do." He came up behind me and stood in the open doorway. "You're so goddamn close to a normal life."

I nodded and wiped my eyes with the heels of my hands.

"Sean..."

"Yeah?" I couldn't stop scrubbing my face, like I could erase what I'd become if I just tried a little harder.

"I don't want you turning tricks anymore. At all."

I dropped my hands and stared at his reflection in the mirror. He wouldn't look at me. "We have to eat."

Gavin moved to sit on the bed, his back to the mirror. "I can take care of us."

"What?" I spun around. "Why is that up to you? We said we'd stick together. No matter what. That means we're in this *together*."

Gavin hadn't moved. The tension was back, his body held still like he was afraid of spooking a wild animal who'd run us both down if given a good enough incentive. Or maybe he was the animal and was afraid he'd scare himself. Or me.

When he spoke again his voice was tight, the words barely making it out past the restrained emotions he couldn't hide from me. "I can't stand it anymore. Can't stand that you're being used. Can't stand the thought of someone else touching you, someone else's cock in your mouth—" He shook his head. "If it was some guy you loved that'd be different, but like that..." He gave another shake.

Maybe the future I wanted with him wasn't so far out of my reach. Maybe he'd been feeling everything I had since I'd met him.

"And you think I can stand it when it's you?"

He turned my way, hope in his green eyes like I'd never seen before, and I knew…

He was feeling everything I was.

"Gavin…"

He said nothing, just searched my face like he wanted to find the answer to every fucked-up situation he'd ever been in, and every fear and doubt he'd ever had.

I went to him. I didn't even think about my actions, just did what I'd always wanted to do, what felt right, like breathing. I straddled his lap, my knees settling on the bed on either side of him.

He looked away as he rested a hand on each of my thighs, the touch gentle and nervous at the same time.

"Gavin."

When he didn't move, I glanced in the direction of his gaze and found him watching me in the mirror through the open bathroom door.

I held his face in my hands and turned him to me. "Gavin, talk to me."

"I…" He slowly ran his palms up my thighs, over my hips to my lower back. The pressure of those hands against my body increased, and he dragged me closer. My legs opened wider and I slid up his lap, our bodies coming together in a way we'd never done before.

I couldn't stop watching those green eyes that were saying much more than I'd ever imagined I'd see from him. Much more than I'd dreamed, even.

He opened his mouth to speak, hesitated, licked his lips as he kept his focus on mine. Finally, he met my stare. "I love you, Sean." He held on to me and flipped us around until my back was pressing into the mattress, his body molded to mine. "I fucking love you. Always have." He ran a palm along my cheek and caressed my lower lip with the pad of his thumb. "Just once I want something real. Something beautiful with you."

Was I still asleep, dreaming while he showered?

He cupped the back of my head and leaned down, then paused with our mouths an inch apart. "Tell me to stop."

Right. I'd get right on that.

I wasn't sure I could breathe much less say something utterly ridiculous like *stop*. No matter what I'd been picturing for the past year, I hadn't hoped for anything even close to this moment, to hear those words from him.

He came the rest of the way and brushed his lips against mine. The soft kiss had a tender quality to it I'd never known possible, so different from the intimacy—or lack of—I'd had in my life.

He swept his lips over mine again. Then the kiss—and the moment—was about so much more as he opened his mouth and his tongue came out to caress my bottom lip. Instinctively, I followed suit. Our tongues met and the kiss deepened. We were wrapped up in each other, his scent and touch were all over me, all around me, like the air I breathed.

He rolled onto his back and pulled me on top of him as he went. One hand at the back of my head, the other across my lower back, he kept me close as the kiss became more intense, more passionate. His every touch spoke of love and devotion even more than his words had.

Although, hadn't his actions said those same things for a long time now? I hadn't wanted to let in the hope that he felt for me the way I did for him, but now I couldn't deny it any longer.

He kissed me again. And again. Nothing cold or rushed or detached.

Then I was on my back again, Gavin holding himself over me. He slid a hand under the front of my T-shirt, those warm fingers caressing their way up my abs and chest. He dropped his lips to my stomach and kissed along the same path, raising my shirt higher as he went.

"God," he said. "I've waited so long to taste you, to touch you."

His words and actions were my own thoughts come to life as he continued to explore my body, peeling off my shirt first, then my pants. Lastly, so very slowly, he gripped the top of my underwear. He stilled with the waistband in his hand. "Tell me to stop."

"You better not."

He smirked. "You want me?"

"You have no idea."

"Yeah, I do." He peeled my underwear over my hips, down my legs, planting kiss after kiss along my skin.

As soon as he had my underwear off, I grabbed him by the back of the neck and pulled him down to me.

He searched my face. I'd never seen him look so...*scared* was the only word that came to mind, and it occurred to me that maybe he'd been as unsure about my feelings for him—if they went beyond friendship—as I'd been about him. Maybe he'd been worried he'd read too much into the way I looked at him, as I feared I'd read too much into the way he trusted me and let me into his life like he'd done with no one else.

"Gavin, tell me you know I love you too."

I caught the smile that hit his lips right before his mouth closed over mine.

The next kiss wasn't slow or soft. It curled my toes and had my body, my every nerve ending, on fire and alive. Gavin sat up on his knees and pulled his T-shirt off. I followed him up and helped him with his jeans.

The touch of his naked body along mine as we settled on the bed again had me feeling like a virgin—like someone who'd never known such a beautiful, basic connection of two people.

He still smelled of the coconut soap. His warm fingertips caressed my skin everywhere, like he couldn't get enough of me. I was so much more than a cock or an ass or a mouth to him.

I arched up into the touches. Everything was new and intoxicating, being touched by someone I cared about, someone who cared about me, someone who...loved me.

Gavin loved me.

His mouth found mine again. Our cocks came together, and I'd never been so relieved and excited to feel a man's erection—to know he really did want me, that we could do this, that we weren't broken beyond repair, that sex could be about love and desire.

He rocked his body against mine, the kisses as much a part of our connection as any other point along our bodies where we came together.

I didn't want the moment to end.

Too bad my body was rushing toward release like I hadn't reveled in this much in a long time. Hell, ever.

I spread my legs and tugged on him. "Gavin…"

He nodded and pulled back. "They in the dresser?"

"Yeah."

He got off the bed and went for the drawer, advancing with that focused determination I loved, but this time, I got to see him move without any clothes blocking the way, the muscles of his ass and thighs flexing with each step.

I sat up on my elbows. "Fuck, you're beautiful."

He came back with lube and a condom. He tossed them on the bed and lowered his body to mine. "Gotta say, kid, you're the one here who's beautiful."

He kissed me, and I opened myself up to him in every way.

It was slow and sweet and over too fast. When he came inside me, he had his hands clasped in mine on the bed, his gaze locked on my eyes, and I knew it was a beginning, not an ending.

* * * *

We made love twice that night. As corny as that sounded, I couldn't call it anything else. Not even in my head.

It hadn't been sex. Hadn't been fucking.

Afterwards, when I had stopped shaking from the enormity of emotions running through me—along with the desire and release—we lay on our sides, his chest to my back, his long body curled protectively, tenderly around mine.

"You okay?" he asked as he leisurely ran his hand over the short hair above my ear.

"Oh God, yeah. Better than okay." I hesitated before saying more. I never felt this insecure or unsure around him, but this moment could change everything for us.

Who was I kidding? It already had.

"Are *you* okay?" I asked.

He sat up and tugged on me until I was on my back looking up at him. "I've never felt this way about anyone." He searched my eyes. "Sean, I want to give you everything, and I've got nothing to give."

"You have you. Us, this, what we just did, it's all I've dreamed of this past year."

He laughed. "You need bigger dreams."

I reached between us and gripped his cock. "I don't think so. Feels pretty big to me."

He laughed with me, rolling us around until we were wrestling and tickling each other. The laughter felt good. Like I was free. Alive.

He stopped us with me on top of him. "I'm serious, you can't give up. You gotta do what that social worker says."

"I will. I am."

He gave a nod, shifted us around again. He kissed his way down my body, laid one kiss after another to my abs, tongued around my bellybutton, and the tips of his hair brushed my skin as he made his way along my flesh. He wasn't trying to turn me on again. He was exploring. Loving.

What I'd been feeling for him was about much more than sex, but now that we'd crossed that line, now that we were here alone, just the two of us, I couldn't deny what I wanted next. Him. Just him for the rest of my life.

No more strangers in public bathrooms or parked cars. No more floating away from myself just so I could live with who I'd become.

Gavin was watching me from where he'd stopped kissing my right hip. "What are you thinking?"

"I don't want to go back."

He slid up the bed and kissed me, a soft, slow caress of his lips across mine. "I know."

I studied his face and the affection in those green eyes. The truth slammed into me. It was written all over him, in every touch between us.

He'd gotten this room so we could be together like this. That's what he'd meant about wanting a memory that lasts.

He wanted this moment to hold on to when things got tough again, when the money ran out, when he was back to sucking some old guy's cock. He really believed he was never going to find a real job, never going to get off the streets, never going to have a normal life.

Even if he couldn't get work, did he think I wouldn't take him with me?

Was he giving up before we'd even had a chance to get started?

I ran the tips of my fingers along his cheek. "Why don't you believe in yourself the way you believe in me?"

"I just gotta be realistic about some things." He let go of me and dropped to the bed. "I've tried. No one is giving a guy like me a job. And if they do, they'll just end up firing my ass eventually. I don't... I don't take orders well."

Which made sense after the foster dad he'd had.

Gavin's cheek twitched with the clench of his jaw. "I won't hold you back."

"You could never do that."

I sat up and tucked my legs under me, feeling young and inexperienced. I'd never had a boyfriend before, never been in love. I didn't know what to say to him. Trusting me with how he felt was a huge step for him, and I didn't want to let him down.

Maybe he would never be able to lean on someone, to rely on them in any way. Maybe he'd never know how to truly accept help, but I had to try. He'd been there for me in so many ways.

"You went off with that guy for a week for us," I said. "And you won't live with me if I'm the one paying for it? That doesn't make sense to me."

He didn't respond. Just kept his stare locked on the ceiling.

"We've gotta start somewhere," I added. "And if I can get us into one of those apartments, there's no way I'm not taking it for us."

Another minute passed before he spoke. "You're taking advantage of my big weakness here."

"What weakness?"

He gave up on the ceiling and met my stare. "There's nothing I wouldn't do for you."

I smiled. I couldn't hold it back. "Does that mean you're gonna live with me?"

He laughed. "We may be homeless, but we've already been living together for a year now."

I rolled my eyes at that, but he was right.

"We're family, Sean. That'll never change."

I bit my lower lip to keep the tears at bay and smacked him right in the middle of his chest.

He flinched. "Ow. What the hell was that for?"

"For being an idiot. You love me and we're family? Then don't start being an ass about money. We get a chance to get the hell out and we're taking it. Together." I stretched out on the bed again and laid my head on his chest.

He wrapped his arms around me and went back to petting my hair. "Okay. We're taking it."

* * * *

Even without a clock, I was very aware of the passage of time. The light of the muted TV cast an eerie glow across the bed, and us. I could tell whenever the latest show had changed to a commercial by that light alone. How many commercial breaks in an hour? In a day? In one week?

Even if I did everything the social worker had said, and even if she did set me up with the interviews she'd promised, we were talking weeks from now, months maybe. She'd mentioned a required deposit and a bank account for the apartment.

What did we do until then? I lifted my head. "I think I should go apply for some jobs while we're staying here. I've got new clothes and someplace to wash up."

Gavin nodded, then said, "Even if you find something this week, it'll take time to save up enough cash to rent a place. And..."

"What?"

"Without that social worker's help, I'm not sure what you'll find."

"It's worth a try. We haven't looked for anything in a while."

"Yeah," he finally said. "You're right. We should try."

I moved to lay my head on his chest again, but before I could settle into place, he sat up and leaned back against the headboard. He was deep in thought, working something out.

"Did you ever have a boyfriend back home?" he asked. "Somebody you'd trust?"

"No." I could feel the blood rush to my face. I pulled again at the loose threads from the weeds on the blanket. "Never had anyone like that. I mean, not even..."

He was watching me again, his eyebrows drawn in like he couldn't believe what I was saying. "So before today, you hadn't..."

I nodded. "I gave a couple blowjobs in high school, but yeah, you were my first." Not really, but he knew what I meant. The first I hadn't been paid for, the first time I'd been fucked by someone who loved me, someone I loved.

He reached out and caressed my face with an open hand. "Is there any chance you can go home?"

I gripped his forearm and stopped his hand's movements. "What?"

"We're not going back to the streets. No matter what." His green eyes never looked so serious, and that was saying a lot. "We have to find a place to stay. I think..." He took a deep breath. "We need someone to help us until we can get on our feet." I couldn't believe he was actually admitting that, but...

"I can't..." I shook my head and swallowed down the panic welling in my throat. "I can't go back there. They hate me. They wanted to *fix me* and when that didn't work..."

He pulled me into his arms.

I was shaking. So was my voice. "Even if they let me in, they'll never let you stay with me."

"It's okay. We'll think of something."

I knew now, that's what he'd been trying to do for weeks.

He tightened the embrace, and I held on to him in return. We sat there in the quiet, listening to the steady drip of water from the shower in the bathroom, like a clock counting down the seconds.

* * * *

I lifted my foot out of the water and used my toes to turn off the faucet. I didn't want to move from where I was leaning back against Gavin's chest, his long legs stretched out on each side of me and his arms wrapped around my chest. The steam-filled bathroom and the warm water surrounding us in the small tub felt like our own private refuge.

After our talk the night before, we'd stayed in bed, neither of us offering anything more about our futures before falling asleep in each other's arms.

In the morning, I'd awoken on my stomach, my right leg tucked up and his mouth doing delicious things to my ass.

When I'd started moaning, he'd flipped me over and took my cock into his mouth. I hadn't been on the receiving end since those rushed exchanges in high school, and when I came between his lips, I had tears in my eyes.

Despite the tub being nowhere near large enough for two people, leaning back against his warm, wet body—his hands caressing my chest, his lips sliding along my neck—was the most romantic moment of my life. I reached back and held his head in my left hand.

He kissed my skin again and again. His lips brushed along my neck to my ear. "I love you," he whispered.

Who knew he'd be the one to say those words first and more often?

I caressed his outer thigh with my other hand and was about to tell him I loved him too when he changed gears on me.

He said, "The only reason either of us haven't gotten really sick is fucking dumb luck. You know that, right?"

"I know." We'd both spent time at the free clinic for treatment of STDs and had been luckier than most that we hadn't gotten something more serious than we had. But I wasn't sure why he'd brought it up. He didn't need to sell me on the reasons we had to change things. He'd already asked me to do the one thing I couldn't—return to my parents' house. What else could he be considering?

He reached over my shoulder for a wash cloth and soaped it up. He encouraged me to lean forward and set to washing my back in slow, sensual strokes. The tropical coconut scent filled the air around us.

"You have cousins, right?" he asked as he continued swirling the wash cloth over my shoulder blades. "Were your aunts and uncles like your parents?"

"Just have the one aunt. Her husband ran out on her when I was little. She's a bitter, hateful person, worse than my mom."

Gavin stopped the washing. He had a hand flat on my back, and I could feel the tension in that one touch.

"What are you thinking?" I asked. We'd come a long way in twenty-four hours. I would've never asked that before if he didn't offer his thoughts on his own.

He still hadn't moved. "That old guy in the SUV..."

The warm air of the bathroom no longer felt relaxing and safe. It felt thick and suffocating. I could barely breathe.

Gavin started scrubbing my back again, his hand working faster than before, like he had to keep moving, had to be doing something. "He wants to see me again. Wants it to be a regular thing."

Now it was me who had to move or I might explode with disbelief and anger and panic. I surged up and stood, the water running down my body onto the floor as I stepped from the tub. On my way out of the bathroom, I found my jeans and tugged them on without underwear. The jeans got stuck twice on my wet skin and I yanked harder.

Gavin came out of the bathroom, a towel around his hips.

I paced along the wall by the hotel room door. "I thought you said—"

"It's good money."

I stilled. "Why? What did he make you do?"

"He just likes to feel young, powerful."

"What did he do to you?" But did it matter? It wasn't anything I wanted him to do with someone else. I couldn't fathom watching him get in that black SUV again. No matter what.

He shrugged and said nothing for so long I was convinced he'd never tell me. Then he said, "He tied me up. Hit me with a leather strap."

My mouth dropped open. I hadn't seen any marks on his body.

He continued like he could hear my thoughts. "Not hard. Barely enough to leave a mark." I almost missed the next words

he said them so low. "Had a scarf around my neck that he…"
Gavin stopped, and I didn't need to hear the rest.

I was back to pacing again, picking up speed the longer I
kept at it. I couldn't imagine him tied up or held down, or
someone hitting him or fucking cutting off his ability to breathe
like that. It wasn't him, even if he was getting paid for it. He
had lectured me enough times not to let myself get into a
situation like that where I couldn't walk away if I needed to.

*Don't ever go off with more than one guy, and never let him
tie you up. A guy gets you tied up, and he'll do whatever the
fuck he wants and you could wind up dead.*

I stopped and faced him. He was staring at that stupid dead-
duck picture over the bed, his lower lip trembling. I moved
toward him. "Gavin…"

He shook his head and took a step back. "It's okay. He's
harmless. Just a lonely old man."

"You can't go back there."

Gavin leaned against the wall behind him, the bed between
us seeming somehow larger than when we'd made love there.
He said, "I don't want you hustling anymore."

"And you're not going to either. We'll figure something
out."

He'd been right. We needed someplace to stay until we
could get jobs and save up some cash.

But we had no one in the city. No family. No friends.

I could think of only one option, one place where I'd once
been liked—loved even.

It was time for me to know the truth.

I sat on the bed and nodded. "How much money do we have
left?"

He searched my face. "Why?"

"Is there enough for two bus tickets to Ohio?"

* * * *

Gavin's eyes were wide as he took in the sight of all the
Christmas lights and lawn decorations at every house we
passed, a light snowfall coming down all around us. When we'd
left the bus station twenty minutes earlier, the snow had started
again. I wasn't sure if that was a good sign or not.

We neared a church, and Gavin stopped in his tracks. "What the fuck is that?"

"Huh?" I followed his gaze. "Oh, it's a live nativity scene. Tells the story of how they believe Jesus was born."

He pointed at the snow-covered lawn before the church where several men and women wearing robes stood in a pile of loose straw under a thin wooden awning that didn't offer much shelter from the falling snow. "Those are real people in costumes?"

"Yeah."

He laughed. So hard I thought he was going to bust something. "Do they know it's freezing out here?"

I laughed with him. "They do it every year."

He jabbed a finger their way again. "That better not be a real fucking baby."

"I think it's a doll." I turned to stand shoulder-to-shoulder with him and watched the live nativity for a minute, Gavin still chuckling beside me. "I guess," I said, "it's supposed to be a tribute to their faith or something."

His laughter cut short. He was quiet as we watched the people standing perfectly still in the snowfall. He took a deep breath and said, "I've never believed in anything that much." He turned my way. "Well, one thing."

I took his hand in mine and squeezed. I wasn't about to hold back, even here. If we couldn't be safe and accepted by most people in this town, then we weren't going to stay for long. Of course, we might not be staying anyway if the two most important people couldn't accept us.

We started walking again, and five minutes later we turned onto Oak Street and headed for the fifth house on the left.

Before we got to the driveway, I stopped short. I couldn't move another inch.

Breathlessly Gavin let out, "Wow." He kept going forward a few more steps, stumbling a bit like he couldn't believe what he was seeing.

The picture of me on the lawn sign was huge and had been altered to advance my age a few years beyond the high school photo from my junior year I could tell it had started out as.

The words above my face read, *Have you seen our grandson?* Beside my huge-ass head was a description of me, when and where I'd last been seen, and a phone number to call.

I wasn't even aware I'd started walking again until I stood beside Gavin at the sign. Gavin lifted a hand and touched the photo of me at the top of my left cheek. "Same eyes," he said.

We kept on standing there in the snow, staring at the sign.

Eventually, he tugged on my arm and led me to the front door. He watched me for a moment, waited, then knocked.

There was no answer.

I couldn't take my gaze off the clear plastic sleeve taped to the door, right at eye level. Inside was an envelope with my name handwritten on the front.

When the silence and my stoic stance continued on, Gavin asked, "That's for you?"

"Yes." That was all I could manage. How long had that envelope been on that door waiting for me? The plastic covering looked like it had been through years of wind and rain and snow.

Gavin carefully slid out the envelope and handed it to me. I read aloud from the folded piece of paper I found inside.

"*Dearest Sean,*

"*If we are gone when you read this, please do not leave. The key to the house is where we always kept it when you were little. Go inside. There's food in the fridge and a room upstairs waiting for you. We love you. Nothing about you and nothing you've had to do since you left will change that. Please do not leave until we can see you.*

"*All our love, Grandma and Grandpa.*

"*P.S. If you're a burglar reading this, yes, there is a key hidden outside. We don't have much but feel free to take a look if you're so inclined, just please put the note back on the door for our grandson.*"

Gavin stared at the paper. "Is that for real?" He sounded in awe.

"Yeah, I think so." That last part was definitely my grandma. So polite, even to someone robbing her.

On shaky legs, I made my way to the planter with the hidden key and unlocked the front door. It was dark inside, but the picture window in the living room offered enough light for us to have a look around. We didn't make it too far before we were stopped again. Boxes of papers were stacked beside the desk in the corner of the living room. I pulled one sheet out of the open top box. The same picture of me, with more details and the number where to call again.

"Look." Gavin picked up a map from the desk. There were red circles and checkmarks across several states with handwritten notes in the margins. "They've been looking everywhere for you."

Fort Wayne. Chicago. Columbus. Pittsburgh.

My hands trembled. Gavin set the map down and retrieved the flyer from me. He gave both my hands a squeeze. "It's okay."

I shook my head and stepped away from him. I moved farther into the living room, not sure where to go or what to do.

Gavin crossed the room and stopped at the Christmas tree in the far corner. Same fake tree with gaps between the branches. It had never looked better. Gavin pointed at the wrapped gifts underneath. "These are for you." He faced me. "All this time, they've been waiting for you to come home."

"I didn't know…" I shook my head again and backed up, panic surging through me. I couldn't breathe. "I…didn't…know…" That they'd accept me, love me no matter what. That I'd had somewhere and someone to turn to three years ago.

Gavin had his arms around me. "It's okay." He tucked my head against his chest and ran a hand over my back. "It's okay."

"Sean?"

At the deep voice across the room, Gavin and I pulled apart.

My grandpa stood at the open front door, his large frame blocking the light outside. He wore a flannel shirt, same as he had when I'd last seen him. He'd lost some weight since I'd been gone, and he'd aged more than seemed possible.

He stepped forward, then stopped like he wasn't sure he should try to come too close or touch me.

For once since we'd arrived at the house, I could move without hesitation. I went to him, and Grandpa wrapped me in his arms. Even at this time of year, he smelled of wet dirt and the fish fertilizer. Like my childhood. I buried my tear-covered face in the flannel shirt. I could hear the tears in his voice.

"I'm so happy to see you."

"I didn't know." I was shaking again.

He held me tighter. "Know what?"

"That you'd love me anyway."

He patted my back. "We'll love you always."

When the tears had subsided and I could finally bring myself to step back, I gestured to Gavin. "Grandpa, this is Gavin."

Grandpa held out a hand. "It's a pleasure to meet you."

Gavin seemed reluctant, like he had no intention of trusting my grandpa until he'd seen more proof that I was wanted—and loved—for who I was.

Finally, Grandpa gave a nod and lowered his hand. He looked to me. "Are you here to stay? In Angola?"

"I'd like to."

He closed his eyes and sighed. When he opened them again, his expression seemed lighter. "We saved you a room upstairs."

"Grandpa, Gavin's not just my friend." I glanced at Gavin, and he gave me a nod of encouragement. "He's my boyfriend and we're in this together."

The tears were back in my grandpa's eyes. Maybe this wasn't such a good idea.

"I thought…" He stopped, seemed beyond words.

"It's okay, Grandpa. I get it. We can go." I signaled to Gavin with a tilt of my head toward the door.

"No!" Grandpa moved fast for how much he'd seemed to have aged. He stepped in our path. "You don't move an inch until your grandmother gets home. Besides, you don't get to run out until I've had my say this time. You think because your parents have treated you horribly that your grandmother and I would react the same way? You didn't give us a chance to tell you how we felt about you being gay. So now's my chance."

I held still. Afraid to go. Afraid of what I'd hear next.

As if he didn't trust me, Grandpa went to close the door, then locked it. He faced us.

Gavin had moved close to stand beside me. He had a hand on my lower back, offering comfort and support I seriously needed right then.

Grandpa moved closer but kept more distance between us than a moment before. "If you think for a minute I don't care about what you do in your personal life—about who you have sex with or fall in love with—then you are sadly misunderstanding what it's like to be a grandparent. I care because I want you to be happy. I want you to have someone in your life who loves you, cherishes you, gives you everything that makes life worth living. Like your grandmother has done for me. And if that's this young man"—he pointed at Gavin—"then I'm beyond thrilled for you." The tears were back. In his eyes and mine. "I thought you were alone this entire time, out there fighting and struggling and not knowing what it felt like to be loved..." He shook his head. "My heart has ached for you every day. If you had only come to us back then..."

I could've erased the last three years of my life.

But then, I wouldn't have met Gavin.

I couldn't fathom thinking about those two outcomes like I had a choice, like I could go back and redo that day I'd walked out.

Because as hard as it would be to leave knowing I had somewhere safe to go where I was loved as every gay kid deserved to be, as hard as it would be to live that life on the streets again, I knew I'd do it all over. I'd do anything to find my way to him.

All I could tell my grandpa was the truth. "He is all that to me."

Grandpa smiled through the tears still wet on his cheeks. He pulled me into another hug, and with his other arm he reached for Gavin, who seemed too shocked to do anything to stop the embrace.

"You're both welcome to stay here for as long as you need or want."

Gavin clutched my forearm. I'd never seen him look like he did right then. Like a little kid. Like unease and disbelief and relief all at once.

I heard someone unlock the front door.

Grandpa looked over his shoulder, still holding Gavin and me in his arms. "He's home to stay. And he's brought someone special for us to meet."

Then there was another pair of arms around me as my grandma kissed my cheek over and over, the four of us laughing and crying.

I was home.

* * * *

I carefully set the glass jars at the bottom of the bag and placed the paper towel rolls on either side, then stacked the two loaves of bread on top. I smiled at the woman paying for her groceries and set to bagging the rest of her items, trying my best not to look like I was paying attention to the two men standing at the far end of the registers.

Gavin was talking with my high school teacher's husband who owned the grocery store, and I could just barely hear them.

The older man's voice sounded kind, compassionate despite his words. "Listen, I don't know you. You've got no job experience, no other references."

Gavin nodded. "I know, but I'll work hard."

"That's what Sean says." He gave a nod as if he'd made his decision, then pointed at Gavin's chest. "Okay, you've got one shot here. Don't mess it up."

The relief on Gavin's face said it all. He wanted the chance, wanted to prove he could stick with a job, that he was worth it. To himself most of all.

He held out a hand and they shook. "Thank you. You won't be sorry."

"Come by on Monday night at eleven. You can start stocking shelves on third with Howard."

Gavin offered his thanks again before the older men stepped away. Then those green eyes found mine as he passed me on his way to the exit.

I finished the last bag for the customer and helped her out to her car with the groceries. When my shift ended an hour later, I walked to my grandparents' house and found Gavin sitting on the edge of the bed in our room.

"Merry Christmas," I said.

He lifted his head and smiled. "Tomorrow's Christmas."

"Maybe for everyone else." Christmas Eve would always be special for me. A year ago, I'd gotten the best gift at the Madison Street Men's Shelter—and not the free condoms and soap.

Gavin's green eyes had a more open, excited spark to them. He gave a nod. He felt the same.

"Did you hear?" he asked.

"Yeah." I straddled his thighs and kissed him. "You have a job."

He wrapped his arms around me and buried his face in my chest. "He's only giving me a chance because of you."

"That's called a reference. Everyone uses them." I held his head in my hands and tugged on him until he looked up at me. "It's okay to accept help. Besides, you'll impress him in no time."

He ran his hands up my back. "No one's ever believed in me the way you do."

"Ditto." I pressed my lips to his cheek, then ran them farther back to his ear. "No one's ever loved me the way you do."

His hands stilled on my back. "Will you ever be able to forget that life?"

I shook my head. "I don't want to. It's how I know what I want with you now. It's how I know what kind of life I want us to build together."

He let go of me and flopped back onto the bed. "That's a shitty way to learn that lesson."

"Yeah." I leaned down to him and laid my cheek against his

chest. "But it doesn't have to ruin us or define us, and it doesn't mean we don't deserve this."

He folded his arms around me again. "I should have taken better care of you. I can't stand the thought of what you—"

I sat up and put a finger over his lips, silencing him. "Stop. It's over. We did what we had to and now we move on. We'll take care of each other as best as we can, just like we've always done."

He nodded and sat up. Slipping his hands under my shirt, he caressed the skin at my sides.

That touch almost distracted me from the other topic I wanted to bring up.

"Did you see?" I asked.

"See what?" He had my shirt raised higher and was running his lips over and around one of my nipples. Then his tongue got in on the act. I lost concentration fast.

"Stop." I squirmed and laughed. "I can't think when you do that."

"Is that bad?"

"Uh-huh."

Another press of his lips to my nipple.

"Maybe," I said.

A lick.

"Or maybe not." Despite that revelation, I pulled him away and forced him to look at me. "Did you see under the tree downstairs? Grandma and Grandpa added more presents."

"They're pretty damn happy you're home."

I shook my head. "The gifts aren't for me. They're for you." I leaned in and whispered in his ear. "You're home now too."

He made like he was going to kiss me but stopped short. "I was home before we even got here." He pointed to the ceiling. Mistletoe hung from a hook above the bed. "Your grandpa gave it to me. Said when you kiss someone under the mistletoe, it's a promise of marriage, that you'll have a happy, long life together."

My heartbeat sped up as Gavin pulled me down to the bed with him. This kiss reminded me of that first one in the hotel room, like he'd been waiting his whole life for this moment.

Or maybe because of all we'd been through, every moment together would be cherished. Maybe we'd never take each other for granted. Maybe we were luckier than most people who never knew what it was like to be so cold and hungry you'd do anything to make it stop. Or to be so truly alone you were afraid you'd disappear.

Gavin kissed me again, then pulled back. "Thank you."

"For what?"

"For giving me something to believe in."

I searched his green eyes.

"Myself," he added.

"You deserve to."

I kissed him and we made love under that mistletoe. If one kiss meant we were destined to be together all our lives, then we'd cinched that deal over and over again by the time we lay curled up in each other's arms.

And that was just fine by me. I could handle being with him forever and then some.

ABOUT THE AUTHOR

Sloan Parker writes passionate, dramatic stories about two men (or more) falling in love. She enjoys writing in the fictional world because in fiction you can be anything, do anything—even fall in love for the first time over and over again. Sloan lives in Ohio with her partner and their neurotic cats. Her greatest moments in life are spent with her family, her friends, and her characters.

To contact Sloan, find out about her other books that are available for purchase, and read free stories, visit: www.sloanparker.com. If you'd like to be notified of new releases and get exclusive sneak peeks, be sure to sign up to receive Sloan Parker's newsletter via her website.